A SUITOR FOR REBEKAH

ENDORSEMENTS

"A STORY ABOUT FINDING LOVE AND JOY AGAIN AFTER AN UNEXPECTED TRAGEDY ROCKS AN AMISH FAMILY'S LIFE. SWEET, COMPELLING, AND FILLED WITH A CHARMING CAST OF CHARACTERS WHO WILL RESONATE WITH READERS OF ALL AGES."
  - SUZANNE WOODS FISHER, BESTSELLING AUTHOR OF *THE QUIETING*

"RACHEL MILLER'S LOVE FOR THE AMISH PEOPLE AND CULTURE IS EVIDENT IN HER STORY."
  - RUTH REID, BESTSELLING AUTHOR OF THE *HEAVEN ON EARTH* NOVELS

"FILLED WITH CHARMING CHARACTERS AND EMOTIONAL MOMENTS THAT WILL TOUCH YOUR HEART. HIGHLY RECOMMENDED FOR AMISH ROMANCE LOVERS!"
  - JENNIFER BECKSTRAND, AUTHOR OF *RETURN TO HUCKLEBERRY HILL*

"MILLER CREATES STORIES OF FAITH, HOPE, AND LOVE THAT DRAW IN THE READER—AND WON'T LET GO... I WAS CAPTURED FROM THE START AS I FOUND MYSELF WEEPING ALONG WITH LEAH."
  - NAOMI MILLER, AUTHOR OF THE BESTSELLING *AMISH SWEET SHOP MYSTERY* SERIES

"MILLER HAS PENNED AN AMISH TALE GUARANTEED TO CAPTIVATE THE READER. THE STORY IS RICH WITH HOPE OF NEW LIFE AND LOVE. A WELL-WRITTEN STORY FOR FANS WHO CAN'T GET ENOUGH BONNET FICTION."
  - LAURA V. HILTON, AUTHOR OF *THE AMISH WANDERER* (WHITAKER HOUSE)

"A COMFORTABLE READ. IT'S A SIMPLE STORY OF FAITH AND THE NEVER-ENDING CYCLE OF LIFE AMONGST THE AMISH... A PLEASANT READ, A STORY WRITTEN WITH COMPASSION."
  - READERS' FAVORITE [4 STARS]

A SUITOR FOR REBEKAH

WINDY GAP WISHES
BOOK TWO

Rachel L Miller
Naomi Miller

He that loveth not, knoweth

not God; for God is love.

~ 1 John 4:8

For Mom

A NOTE FROM THE AUTHORS

Hello lovely reader,

Thank you for picking up our novel. We hope you enjoy reading about our made-up family as much as we have enjoyed writing about them.

Yes, as sad as it is and as much as we wish they were real, the characters and the communities in the following story are entirely fictional.

While there are Amish communities both in Cattaraugus County in New York and Holmes County in Ohio, we have created our own fictional communities within those areas so that we do not accidentally imitate any actual members of the Amish community.

Also please note that each community lives by slightly different rules and standards so we may have taken a bit of creative license in certain areas to make portions of our story work. Please understand that this is done, not out of a lack of research or respect, but strictly in the interest of the story itself.

God bless!

~Naomi & Rachel

GLOSSARY

The German/Dutch dialect spoken by the Amish is not a written language. It is solely dependent on the location and origin of each settlement. The spellings below are approximations.

Ach = Oh (exclamation)
Aenti = Aunt
allrecht = all right
appeditlich = delicious
boppli/bopplin = baby/babies
bruder/bruders = brother/brothers
danki = thank you
Dat = Dad
daudi haus = house for grandparents
Dietsch = Pennsylvania Dutch
dochder/dochdern = daughter/daughters
eiferich = excited
Englisch/Englischer = non-Amish person
freind/freinden = friend/friends
frau = wife
froh = happy
gegisch = silly
Gotte = God
Gotte's wille = God's will
grandkinner = grandchildren
grossdaddi = grandfather
grossmammi = grandmother
Gudemariye = Good morning

gut = good

Gut nacht = Good night

haus = house

hochmut = pride

in lieb = in love

jah = yes

kaffe = coffee

kapp = head covering

kind/kinner = child/children

kumme = come

lecherich = ridiculous

maedel/maedels = girl/girls

Mamm = Mom

naerfich = nervous

nee = no

nacht = night

Onkel = Uncle

Ordnung = rules for Amish life

rumschpringe = running around time for youth

schmaert = smart

schpassich = odd

schweschder/schweschders = sister/sisters

sitzschtupp = special living room

verrickt = crazy

verhuddelt = mixed up/confused

Was iss letz = What's wrong

Wie geht's = How are you?

wunderbaar = wonderful

PROLOGUE

Rebekah woke to the sound of *Mamm's* sobbing. She leaned up on her elbow, rubbing a hand over her eyes in an attempt to clear them of sleep. She looked around the room, trying to figure out where *Mamm* was, but there was no light to help her and only erratic sobs to latch onto. She sat up, trying to wake herself up enough to focus better... and then it hit her.

Dat's gone. That could be the only explanation for *Mamm's* broken-hearted sobbing.

He must have slipped away while she was at the hospital earlier with Onkel Joel. He had come to collect *Mamm* and they had gone off to the hospital hours ago.

Grossmammi had stayed with Rebekah for a long

time, but someone had come to the door to tell her that she needed to come to the hospital, too. So she had left and *Grossdaddi* had stayed with her.

Now *Mamm* was back and terribly upset. The only thing that could mean was that *Dat* was gone. Rebekah sat there a moment trying to think about it, but her sleep-muddled mind couldn't seem to handle it so she just sat there, staring into the darkness, listening to *Mamm* cry.

· · ·

Naomi woke with a start! She sat up and looked around her. It only took a moment to see where she was, with the bright sunshine streaming in through the nearby windows. She glared at the sunshine. Why should it be so bright and normal today? The sky should be dark and stormy; at least it would match the emotions thrashing around inside of her.

She looked over at Rebekah's bed only to see that it was empty. She didn't remember falling asleep; she certainly had not meant to fall asleep on the floor of her *dochder's* room. Rebekah must have gone downstairs to help her *Grossmammi* with breakfast hours ago. And no doubt *Dat* was out somewhere helping Joel with the chores.

Where is everyone? What time is it? Why did they just leave me here on the floor? She scolded herself immediately for her thoughts. Rebekah may have tried to wake her up, but been unable to. She certainly would not have been able to get her *Mamm* off the floor.

It was then that she noticed the blanket draped over her and her hand was touching something soft. Looking over to where her hand was, she saw Rebekah's pillow on the floor where her head had been only a minute ago.

Warmth spread through her at the thoughtfulness of her young *dochder*. She had not been able to wake Naomi up or move her, but she had done everything she could to make her spot on the floor more comfortable. That warmth chased away the anger and resentment that was churning within Naomi and exposed what she had been trying to hide behind them —the heartbreak.

Oh, he's gone. He's really gone now. What am I going to do? How will we go on without him? The tears came again, flooding her eyes, and she could feel the sobs wracking her shoulders. She lay back down, her head nestled on the pillow, and pulled the blanket up to try and muffle the sounds of her sobs.

It would be a long time until she would be able to face anyone else. She had a moment to be thankful her

Mamm and *Dat* were about somewhere. They could take care of Rebekah for a few minutes more.

The dearest things of life are mostly near at hand.

~ Amish Proverb

ONE

Rebekah looked out the window at the small buildings in town as they rode through. It was such a tiny place. Not that Hope Springs had been a booming metropolis, but it was larger than what she had seen here so far.

She hadn't seen anything in this town or any other they had driven through to be excited about. And she still couldn't believe *Mamm* had insisted she come back to the house with them.

All I wanted to do was visit with Aenti Ida and the cousins. I have not gotten to spend any real time with them in years...

Mamm had spoken rather sharply to her when she'd

argued that she should be allowed to stay with *Aenti* Ida for a few days, so she was determined to sit here and be as quiet as possible.

Maybe they will just forget that I am here. She sat there just like that, as Samuel drove the buggy, listening to her *Mamm* talk to him about silly things, looking out the tiny window at the scenery around them as they drove past.

Don't know what is supposed to be so interesting about more snow... especially when there's so much of it, you can't see anything but a blanket of white everywhere.

The silent tirade went on in her head for a long time as they rode through the snowy countryside between Windy Hill and Windy Gap. She sat there with her arms crossed over her chest and pouted silently.

When she caught sight of another tiny town coming into view, she sat looking out the window on her side, thinking how small and uninteresting the town was. There were only a few shops, and none of them that *Mamm* had mentioned sounded one bit appealing to her. The only redeeming quality she knew of so far was that several of them were run by plain folk. At least that would mean *Mamm* would allow her to visit them without her.

If I ever get to go into town... besides, why would

anyone want to go into town in such cold weather?

Just then they passed a large parking area that looked specially made for buggies, and she noticed a young man standing on the sidewalk.

He had stopped and was standing there with his head tilted up to the sky. Something about the expression on his face caught her attention and she found herself wondering if he was enjoying the snow or if perhaps there some delicious smell in the air that she couldn't enjoy from inside the enclosed buggy.

As she watched him, hoping that his clean-shaven face meant more than just that he was unmarried, she couldn't help noticing how handsome he was. From the raised height of the buggy, she could see his face clearly even though it was tilted up. Perhaps that was what made it easier to see how attractive his features were.

His face was not soft or smooth, but weather worn and rugged, but somehow that made him all the more appealing to her. She was almost afraid to hope that he might be her age.

None of the boys my age look like that in Hope Springs. He doesn't look like a boy to me... he looks like a man.

She kept her nose pressed to the tiny window as they moved past the parking area where he stood, attempting to keep him in sight as long as possible.

After a moment more, he lowered his head and began walking toward one of the shops. As he entered the shop, she looked at the name over the door and was excited to see a plain, wood sign. That was very *gut* news indeed.

Perhaps there is something in town I would be interested in after all.

Rebekah quickly stifled the giggle that tickled her throat. She would not want *Mamm* asking what she found so funny.

She would most certainly think I am being rude or perhaps I was making fun of the town.

Rebekah suddenly realized that her feelings had changed in the past few moments. She was glad that she had come with them, like *Mamm* had wanted. If she had stayed at *Aenti* Ida's house, she would not have seen the young man and the store he went into and, knowing that, now she could hardly wait to *kumme* back into town.

But how will I convince Mamm to let me kumme back into town today? She will only think I am trying to find some excuse to not be with her and our new family.

She thought about it as they left the town behind and drove along the smooth, narrow country lanes. As more time passed, Rebekah realized that it would likely be silly to *kumme* back into town today to find the young man. He would likely be long gone by the time they got back to the farm and she could manage to come up with a *gut* enough reason to return. She would have to wait for another day.

She focused her thoughts on the name of the shop he had walked into. She would need to make sure to remember it.

Sew Sweet—what an odd name for a store. Why would that be the name? Did that mean they sold sewing supplies or sweets? Had the sign-maker spelled the word wrong?

She wanted to ask, but Leah was still looking out her window and *Mamm* was still talking to Samuel, who raised a hand to wave every time they passed plain folk along the road.

Leah knows him! The thought came to her quickly and she turned to ask Leah who he was, but just as quickly, another thought occurred to her.

Ach. He knows Leah. Has probably known her forever. They've grown up together. Why would he even look twice at me when she's right here, where she has always been? With that thought, she turned and looked straight ahead, blinking away the tears that had suddenly sprang to her eyes.

Well this is no different than how things were back home. The anger that had sustained her all this time began to melt away and misery crept in behind it.

Would things ever be different, and did it truly matter where she was if her life was meant to be the same wherever she lived? She looked up at the roof of the buggy, trying for a moment to blink away the tears that were threatening to spill over.

Why, Gotte... why did I have to come so far to be in the exact same situation?

It is not fair. She leaned back against the seat again and crossed her arms over her chest and gave up trying to stop the tears that were spilling silently down her cheeks.

. . .

It had been several hours. Naomi was still fighting tears, although they were much closer to winning now than she was. She had thought it would be just she and Samuel and Rebekah who took her parents to the train station, but nearly everyone had ended up going along with them. No one had wanted to miss out on one more chance to say goodbye.

They had ended up taking three buggies and there was no telling what the sight of them had set people to thinking as they made their way from Windy Gap, through Windy Hill, on to Clearview and then to the train station.

The goodbyes had been much more emotional than Naomi had expected, too. All of the *kinner*, Leah especially, had become very attached to their new grandparents and had been reluctant to see them go.

Rebekah on the other hand, had been almost angry. She had been quiet all morning, sullen on the drive to the station and downright rude when it came time to say goodbye to her grandparents.

Everyone else had come back again and again for more hugs and to tell *Grossmammi* and *Grossdaddi* "...one more thing" but Rebekah had stood away from the group. Naomi had practically had to drag her *dochder* over to tell her grandparents goodbye.

Naomi had started to correct Rebekah once her parents had finally boarded the train, but she had been distracted by a slight pressure on her elbow. She'd looked behind her to see Samuel shaking his head slightly.

He then leaned in to whisper quietly in her ear. "Let it be for now, dearest. She is dealing with a lot. Let's give her a little more time before we lose patience with her."

To say that Naomi had been surprised to realize that Samuel had such insight into Rebekah—especially something that she had clearly missed—was more than understating the situation. Seeing the wisdom in his words, she had nodded her head and then leaned against his shoulder as she watched her parents wave from the train window, feeling immeasurably blessed to have married such a wonderful man.

Gotte had truly had both of their best interests in mind when He had brought them together.

Now, driving toward their new home, Naomi watched Rebekah out of the corner of her eyes as she chatted with Samuel. For a minute, while they were in town, she had actually looked interested... even happy. What had happened to change her back so quickly into the sullen, young *maedel* who was such a stranger to Naomi?

What exactly did I miss all those years, when I was busy taking care of John and trying to keep everything together... all the time not realizing that everything was falling apart?

Mamm and *Dat* had never said anything about Rebekah having a rough time with the other young people. Naomi tried to tell herself that her parents had only been doing what they thought was best for her and Rebekah... when they continued to urge her to marry Joel, and even when it came to not understanding when she told them she had to get away from their home for a time, but it did not make sense that they would not have told her what was going on with her own *dochder.*

Perhaps they thought it best not to mention it with everything else I had going on then... but why not now? John has been gone almost two years. Why did no one tell me what is going on with my own dochder?

With that, the anguish she had been pushing away for too long rose up and washed over her in a wave, nearly drowning her as it churned and slammed into her heart.

I should have known. No one should have had to tell me what was going on. She's my dochder and I missed so much with her that I should not have had to miss.

Her thoughts were interrupted by that same slight pressure on her arm. She looked up into Samuel's concerned face and realized there were tears streaming down her cheeks. She buried her head against his shoulder as the anguish mixed with shame and her hot tears started to fall faster.

"Later," was all she said. She could feel the movement as Samuel nodded his head and shifted slightly, trying to make his position more comfortable for her.

She scooted over on the bench a little, to get closer and then she closed her eyes and began to pray, but she didn't move again until she felt the bump that meant they had left the smooth pavement and were on their own drive. Saying a silent *"Amen"* she opened her eyes and sneaked a glance back at the *maedels.*

Leah was still looking out the window, smiling as they drove along the rock covered drive. Rebekah was still sitting much as she had for most of the trip, arms crossed over her chest and a look on her face of anger and disinterest. There were no fresh tears on her cheeks but her eyes were still a bit red around the edges.

Naomi had no idea what to do for for her *dochder,* but she knew she could not ignore Leah or any of the other *kinner* in favor of Rebekah. And, as much as she would like to spend extra time with her *dochder,* she knew no amount of time would make up for what she had missed out on already.

All she could do now was try and move forward with a different approach. To try to make certain she did not miss anything else.

TWO

Rebekah looked out the window at the unfamiliar sights. Everywhere she looked, there was snow. The yard was buried beneath at least a foot of it and so were the fields beyond. It seemed fitting that the landscape out her window—for all of it's differences—was so much like the one she had seen from her own window at home.

Home. I guess this is home now, so I should probably get used to it.

She knew her thoughts were uncharitable but she couldn't help it and wasn't sure she wanted to. All of this had happened so quickly. Even though she had been determined not to stop *Mamm* from finding happiness, she found that the changes were a much larger shock than she had expected.

There wasn't even all that much she could do to occupy her time. *Mamm* had taken over most of the cooking and baking. Leah and Lillian did the laundry and the other cleaning. They had all told her to take some time to adjust to being here and to relax. But she didn't want to relax. She wanted to be doing something... anything. She had to find something to do that would take her mind off everything she'd left behind—or she just might scream!

Trying to distract herself, Rebekah looked back out at the yard. She could see several sets of tracks going to and from the barn. The boys must be out helping their *dat* with the morning chores.

She hadn't been able to even think about calling him *Dat* yet. He had told her she could call him Samuel or *Dat,* whichever one she was comfortable with, but she had tried hard to simply speak to him, without using any form of address. He was a *gut* man and she didn't want to hurt him if she could avoid it. It wasn't his fault that she was having difficulty adjusting to the situation.

Determined to find something to do, she got up and headed downstairs. She'd been sitting here for a half hour at least, dressed and trying to figure out exactly how she was supposed to relax. She would find something to do downstairs.

She had to.

. . .

Naomi looked up with a smile when Rebekah walked into the kitchen. She could hear Leah humming as she stopped in the *mudroom* to take off her wet boots. And Rebekah was standing there in front of her with a scowl on her beautiful face.

Without saying a word to anyone, Rebekah turned and walked out of the room and headed back up the stairs. At the sound of her bedroom door slamming, Naomi winced.

Oh, how I wish I knew what to do to help her. Please Gotte, help me to know what I can do to make this easier for Rebekah.

Naomi had repeated the same prayer countless times over the past few weeks, but nothing seemed to be making a difference. She had told herself Rebekah just needed time, but that certainly didn't seem to be helping, either. Eventually she was going to run out of patience with her *dochder.* Everyone around her was making an effort to include her in the family, but Rebekah was returning none of it.

She had been so certain Rebekah would be thrilled to have a *schweschder* the same age and so many other *bruders* and *schweschders* around her. Rebekah had asked so many times as a child why she didn't have any *bruders* and *schweschders* of her own. Naomi had tried to explain that her *dat's* illness made it impossible for them to have more *kinner,* but it was a difficult thing for a young *maedel* to understand.

Now of course, she was surrounded by family and she didn't seem to even want to try to get to know them.

Perhaps I can talk to Leah about it. Maybe she can do something to draw her out. Though Naomi didn't really want to continue to ask Leah to go out of her way to help Rebekah or to keep making excuses for her.

What can I do to help her find her place here?

Naomi thought about the young people in the area and remembered that Leah had told her it would be another two weeks before there would be another gathering of the youth, on account of the weather.

After the wedding, a blizzard had hit the area. No one went anywhere, including church or youth gatherings, for nearly a month. Being stuck indoors mostly hadn't improved Rebekah's disposition in the least. Perhaps if she had been able to get out and make some new friends it would have been easier on her.

As it was, Rebekah's unhappiness was wearing thin on a few members of the family, including her *mamm.*

I suppose I should have more patience with Rebekah. Even I'm having trouble adjusting—and this was my idea.

. . .

Rebekah watched as *Mamm* walked upstairs with Lillian. For just a moment, she had thought things might actually be different here. But she should know by now how silly that was. She wasn't going to have a life here that was any different from how things had been in Ohio.

Feeling let down to have one bright and shining moment of possibility, only to have it to be snatched away from her, she allowed the anger and misery to wallow within her as she followed slowly up the stairs and made her way to the bedroom she would share with Leah.

I will just sit here until it is time for dinner.

No one around here seemed to need her help anyway.

The sadness pressed in on her as she plopped down on the bed. How could she have thought it would be different here? She was still the odd one out, the one who was different from everyone else, the one whose *Mamm* never had any time for her.

Everyone back in Hope Springs had been certain her *Dat* must have committed some terrible sin to be sick for so long and never be healed. Even the fancy doctors had not been able to help him, but Rebekah had been certain *Dat* would never have done anything to deserve such a thing. For awhile she had even been angry with *Gotte* for allowing him to be sick.

She had always thought it ironic that the person who convinced her *Gotte* was not to blame happened to be *Englisch.* Even more ironic was that her explanation had made so much more sense than anything she had heard from those in their plain community about how *Gotte* worked.

Rebekah was grateful for it and she had found herself spending more and more time at their local library where she had a chance to talk to the woman. The library was one of the few places she could go where no one questioned her behavior. Over the years it had become a sanctuary for her. She had spent many hours getting lost in the books there.

She never felt the need to apply for a library card, which had given her the perfect excuse to sit and read as long as she wanted—and as often as she could.

During her school days, she would stop at the

library on her way home and stay until they closed. When she was done with school, Rebekah had begun visiting the library anytime she could find the time. She had spent many an hour strolling along the aisles, glancing at the shelves and reading the titles on the book spines.

She had discovered many different worlds inside the pages of fiction books, as well as learning much from the non-fiction sections. Learning had been much encouraged when she had been in school, but Rebekah had noticed that while most of the other scholars were only interested in learning what was necessary, she had been intrigued and wanted to know more. It had been yet another reason to make her way to the library over the years.

Thinking of her beloved library made her wonder if she had missed seeing one in Windy Gap when they had driven through town earlier. She had been focused on the one side of the street. Perhaps it was on the other side of the street or one of the few side streets that she had seen branch off.

I can ask Leah. Maybe she will even take me. The thought took hold of her and gave her the tiniest glimmer of hope. There would be no competition among the books. And oh, wouldn't it be wonderful if Leah shared her love of reading. They could go to the library together and read.

She thought about what little she knew of her new *schweschder,* wondering what sort of books Leah preferred. She constructed a scene in her head where they would discover that they enjoyed the same books and they would sit for hours and talk and talk and talk about all the same stories they loved.

Suddenly excited, she bounced up off of her bed and rushed out of the bedroom and nearly ran down the hall as she got caught up in her excitement. Turning at the top of the stairs, she forced herself to walk slower... and then she heard the shouting.

. . .

Samuel stumbled into the kitchen with Caleb leaning heavily on him. He was mumbling something over and over, but the words were impossible to understand. From the scene he had found, it wasn't hard to discern what had happened. Now he just needed to figure out if he would need to get Caleb to a doctor or if they could handle whatever had happened here.

He called out for Naomi and Leah, then added a general shout for anyone who was nearby. Immediately, the pounding of feet could be heard from every direction.

Gut.

They all knew it was serious when he raised his voice.

While he was waiting for everyone to join him in the kitchen, he helped Caleb into a chair and then pulled another one close to place his blood-soaked leg onto. When he moved Caleb's leg, his son let out a strange sound that was part cry and part groan. Samuel grit his teeth, knowing that the pain would not get any better for his son, especially since he must determine the extent of Caleb's injuries quickly. Time was not on their side.

When Caleb nodded at him, knowing—even through the pain—what his *dat* must do, Samuel turned his attention to the leg he had just propped up. There was blood soaking the lower part of Caleb's right pant leg so Samuel focused his attention there. There was already a long cut in the pants so he pulled his pocket knife out and carefully cut the fabric the rest of the way down. What he saw surprised him and he struggled to control his reaction.

He had expected a cut, a gash even, but the length of the cut in Caleb's pants had not prepared him for the reality of the wound. He could never have expected the shape that Caleb's leg was in.

We are definitely going to need a doctor.

Naomi appeared at his shoulder and then rushed away again. He expected to hear the water running, but he never imagined what happened next. Behind him, he heard Naomi's sweet voice issuing orders to the other *kinner* in a tone of velvet steel.

She sent Leah to get several large bath towels. She sent Matthew to get his *bruders* from the barn. She sent Lillian to gather several old blankets that were thick and clean, and she repeated *clean* for Lillian, putting special emphasis on the word. A moment later he heard three pairs of feet run off. He was also surprised to hear her say a moment later. "*Gut*. Rebekah, come and help me."

Then she appeared again at his side, this time with several wet kitchen towels and a small hand towel.

She directed him to gently lift Caleb's leg so that she could slide one of the larger towels underneath it. She then proceeded to wrap the towel tightly around his leg, pushing gently as she did, until she had the sides of the deep gash in his leg nearly closed.

She had folded the smaller towel into a thick pad which she laid directly onto the wound. The next thing she did was to wrap another of the towels around his leg, overlapping the first towel and the thick pad, pulling it up to cover the wound. She did the same with the third towel Rebekah handed her, covering the other side.

He could do no more than watch, amazed at her resourcefulness and her calm. He could feel his insides shaking. He feared he might begin to panic at any moment and here was his tiny *frau,* calm and clear and precise. She didn't even seem to notice the blood that covered the chair and the floor and their clothes as she quickly worked to bind up Caleb's wound.

Leah skidded into the kitchen just then, and stood there balancing the stack of towels as she waited to see what Naomi wanted with them.

"Very *gut,* Leah. You thought to bring the dark brown towels. I had hoped you would, but I didn't think to ask." She turned to take the top towel off the stack in Leah's arms and then she slid it under Caleb's leg and wrapped it tightly over the kitchen towels that were holding the wound together. Caleb let out a grunt of pain as she did it, but she did not stop or loosen the towel at all.

Samuel looked around at the sound of pounding feet coming through the hallway. Benjamin was in the lead with Elam and Peter right behind him. Matthew was not with them, but Benjamin must have seen Samuel's searching glance.

"He is getting the wagon hitched up for us. He told

us enough of what happened and I thought the buggy might be a bad idea." Samuel nodded his head and sent a tight smile in his son's direction.

The boys stood there, still dressed for being outdoors, looking at Caleb—sweating and bleeding and occasionally grunting in pain. Samuel was holding Caleb's leg up for Naomi's ministrations and the others stood by, awaiting instructions.

Samuel could not help but wonder how odd the scene must appear to them, and he had the strangest urge to laugh.

They all breathed a deep sigh of relief when they heard the unmistakable sound of wheels crunching over gravel outside and everyone moved forward in anticipation.

Naomi immediately began issuing orders again. To their credit, the boys looked over at Samuel for his approval before moving to obey, but not one of them argued with Naomi's words.

Between the four of them, they gently lifted Caleb out of the chair, using the towels Leah had brought down. Naomi lifted his injured leg and she was careful to keep it a bit higher than the rest of his body. She also admonished Caleb to be as limp as he could because he might want to help, but if he moved at all, it would only hinder. Samuel could see Caleb gritting his teeth as they moved him, but he was certain it had more to do with the pain he was experiencing than difficulty following Naomi's order.

They carefully made their way out to the wagon that was parked right at the bottom of the stairs. Samuel could see that Matthew had done a very *gut* job of pulling the wagon up. He had even managed to back it up so that they were able to step off the stairs without having to go all the way down and then lift him into the back of the wagon

Samuel made a point to call out to Matthew and tell him what a *gut* job he had done and then he put his concentration into getting Caleb settled into the back of the wagon. Lillian came out the front door then with Rebekah and Leah. They had both taken blankets from her because the stack she had brought was so tall. For some reason the only thing he could think of right then was that she couldn't possibly have been able to see where she was going.

Naomi pulled the blankets, one by one and wrapped them around and over Caleb. Then she stepped back and spoke to the boys.

"Do I need to go with you or can one of you handle the job of keeping pressure on his leg?" Benjamin immediately stepped forward and answered. "I can handle it. I've done this before. Do I need to put pressure on the top or from the sides of his leg?"

"From the top, but not too much. Mostly you need to make sure none of the towels come loose. I've wrapped them tightly enough and there are several layers, but they may try to come loose as the wagon bounces so just keep enough pressure on them to keep everything in place."

And with that, she stepped back. Benjamin nodded sharply before turning and stepping up onto the wagon. Matthew had already scooted over and Elam had taken his place in the driver's seat. Peter and Benjamin arranged themselves to support Caleb as they drove.

Samuel stepped up to Naomi and hugged her tightly, not paying any mind to the blood that covered them both. She hugged him back a moment before giving him a gentle shove.

"Go on now. You need to get him there as fast as you can... safely!" She directed the last word to Elam. Samuel gave her a quick kiss before stepping into the back of the wagon to help his sons and Elam sent the team rumbling down the drive at a fairly quick pace.

THREE

Naomi turned back to look at Leah, Rebekah and Lillian, who were standing on the top step watching the wagon as it bumped its way down the long drive. She hoped they were going slowly enough that Benjamin was able to keep the towels secure around Caleb's leg.

When she reached the top step, she placed one arm around Leah and the other around Rebekah as Lillian turned to wrap her arms around her *schweschders* as well. As a group, they hugged tightly and stood there holding on to each other.

"I want to tell you *maedels* that each of you did a *wunderbaar* job helping. I could not have taken such *gut* care of Caleb without your help. It is *gut* to know you are all so *gelassenheit* in a crisis."

"Will Caleb's leg be alright?" Lillian's voice was very small as she looked up at Naomi, clearly hoping for a positive answer. Naomi did not want to be dishonest, so she chose her words carefully, since she didn't want to scare the young *maedel*.

"He will certainly be better off for our quick response. We must leave him in *Gotte's* hands now. *He* knows what is best for Caleb, for all of us... *jah?*" She left the question hanging and looked down at Lillian, who nodded her head and looked relieved at the same time. It might not be the answer she wanted, but she seemed to be content with it.

They stood there together for several minutes before the cold finally started to register. Naomi gently squeezed Rebekah's and Leah's shoulders as she said, "Let's go inside and get things cleaned up."

Leah laughed in response and Naomi was glad to hear only a little tremor in it. She was also relieved to hear Leah's humor in what she said in return.

"Isn't it just like boys to make a mess, then go off and leave it for us to clean up?" Her words made everyone laugh and Naomi was glad to hear it. The tension was beginning to fade.

Soon they would all feel the effects of it—that she

remembered all too well from her days of caring for John. Much better to get busy now while their energy was still flowing. Later they would all be worn out and not at all up to the energy it would require to get all that blood off the floor.

.   .   .

Rebekah looked up from scrubbing a spot on the floor as Leah walked past carrying a bucket filled with clean water. Her anger and annoyance from earlier was forgotten, replaced by worry and concentration on the task at hand.

She was glad *Mamm* had known a trick to get all the blood out of the rug, off the floor and the chair and out of the tablecloth, not to mention all of their dresses. Hopefully the trick would work on everyone's clothes when they returned from the doctor. She looked up at the clock again to see that it had only moved forward a few minutes.

Shouldn't they be back by now? Was it bad that they were not back yet? It had been hours already.

"*Mamm*, shouldn't they be back by now?" She asked the question as *Mamm* walked back into the kitchen. Naomi had been outside helping Leah and Lillian with the laundry and Rebekah had not wanted to leave this task unfinished to seek her out.

"I just sent Lillian down to the phone shanty to see if there are any messages."

Rebekah waited for more, but *Mamm* kept walking toward the sink and did not say anything else. How could she be so *gelassenheit?* Every minute seemed to last an eternity and Rebekah felt like she might collapse from the strain of not knowing what was happening. "How can you be so *gelassenheit, Mamm*?"

"*Ach,* Rebekah, I am anything but. It may not look that way to you, but the only thing that is keeping me from falling apart right now is staying busy." Naomi walked over to her *dochder* and wrapped her arms around her while she was speaking.

"When your *Dat* was sick, there were many times that I could do nothing but wait. A lot of times I was right there with him and I could help in some way. That made it a little easier to distract myself. But there were also many times I could do nothing, even though I was there with him. It was not an easy time, but it certainly taught me patience." She stopped and took a deep breath.

Rebekah could hear the trembling in her voice now. It was comforting to know that *Mamm* was just as worried as she herself was. Somehow it made her feel better to know she was a part of what was happening.

She found herself worried over this young man who was now her *bruder*.

She barely even knew him and he could be dying right now... Rebekah was surprised at the ache that filled her at that thought. She felt tears fill her eyes and turned her head into *Mamm's* shoulder. "*Mamm*, what will we do if he's not *allrecht?*"

"Rebekah, we cannot think that way. We have to trust that he is in *Gotte's* hands." She moved back a bit and waited until Rebekah looked at her before going on. "Rebekah, do you believe that *Gotte* knows better than we do? Do you believe that He has Caleb in His hands now?"

Rebekah nodded, but knowing did not stop her tears.

"Then we must trust *Him*. Caleb will be well if it in in *Gotte's wille.*" She hugged Rebekah tight again. "*Ach*, I know it's hard, *dochder*. It is not easy for me either, I can assure you of that. This is part of being a *Mamm*. You will understand one day all too soon."

Rebekah thought about that for a moment. To become a *mamm* herself, there would have to be a young man interested enough in her to want to marry her. She thought of the youth gathering Leah had mentioned several times in the past week, which brought to mind the young man she had seen when they were driving through town. He might have known Leah her entire life.

In fact all the young men in the area had most likely known her their whole lives, but Leah could only choose one of them. That would mean there were others who might find themselves interested in her.

It might be worth attending the youth gathering after all.

Suddenly, she felt a glimmer of hope. *Perhaps it will not be such a bad thing, living here where no one knows me, where no one will look at me with pity and sadness.*

It could be a very gut thing indeed.

Rebekah shook herself a little when she realized what *Mamm* had done. She had distracted her and stopped her from worrying, for a few minutes at least. She turned to say *danki* to *Mamm* just as Lillian pushed through the front door. She was waving a piece of paper in the air and she didn't even stop to remove her wet, muddy boots.

"He's okay! He's okay! He's okay!" She finally came to a skidding halt right next them, but she kept saying it over and over in a loud voice full of excitement as she bounced up and down. Rebekah even found herself bouncing a little too as relief coursed through her.

He's going to be allrecht. *Gotte is gut.*

A second later, she heard the dull thud of feet as Leah came rushing down the hall and then practically slid into the kitchen. She had taken the time to remove her boots at the back door and her feet were sliding on the floor in her hurry. Rebekah reached out to catch her before she tumbled and they were both laughing as Lillian continued to prance around the kitchen.

Rebekah sneaked a peek at *Mamm* and was surprised to see tears on her cheeks. She had her face turned up toward the ceiling and her eyes were closed so perhaps she was thanking *Gotte* and the tears were because she was so happy to hear that Caleb would be well.

It was several minutes before anyone calmed down enough to ask Lillian to tell them the rest of the message and even then, *Mamm* had to take it from her because she could not be still long enough to read the words to them.

"Caleb is well. We are blessed to have such a wonderful doctor so close to us. He has worked very hard for a long time to close up Caleb's wound, but he says everything is clean and it looks *gut*. We will be returning home soon." She read the words again silently and then surprised them all by laughing. "I do hope they drive home more slowly."

It only took a moment for everyone to join in with

her and they were all laughing. They came together in the middle of the room in a circle and leaned against each other as they laughed and cried and let all of the tension that had been building up since Samuel walked in supporting Caleb slowly drain away.

After a few minutes, *Mamm* looked around at them and let out a short back of laughter before she stepped away, shaking her head. "Look at us. We are a mess. It looks like we need to clean up again."

Lillian was the first to look down at herself and when she realized she was standing in a puddle of muddy water, bright pink color made its way up her neck and spread out across her cheeks.

"No, Lillian. Don't you be worrying." *Mamm* shook her head at Lillian, gently reassuring her that she was not in trouble. "Any one of us would have done the same if we had been the one to get that message. I am glad you rushed in here to let us all know as quickly as possible." She nodded her head as she spoke and after a moment, Lillian nodded too and the pink in her cheeks seemed to lighten a little.

Leah held out a hand to her so she could step out of her boots and carry them to the mudroom, then they each went their own way, getting the messes cleaned up so the men would come home to a clean house.

.   .   .

Samuel watched the road ahead closely. The light had retreated quickly and he was glad to be the one handling the team. He could hear the boys behind him, talking quietly and there was even an occasional laugh.

It was a surprise to be sure that Caleb felt able to join his *bruders* as they talked and laughed but it was certainly reassuring to hear. Caleb had certainly been in *Gotte's* hands today. All afternoon Samuel had been trying to think of anything but of the many things that could have gone wrong.

If I had not come around the barn when I did...

He stopped that thought. It would do no *gut* to dwell on what might have been. *Gotte* had guided all of their steps and Caleb would be just fine.

That brought Naomi to mind. Samuel could not have known his *frau* would be so cool in a crisis. She'd known exactly what to do for Caleb and had wasted no time getting him on his way to the doctor. She was a blessing to them all for sure and for certain. He was again grateful *Gotte* had brought them together. Suddenly he could hardly wait to get back home and show Naomi just how much he appreciated her.

I just hope she isn't too tired. He laughed as he thought of how tired he was. Naomi had stayed behind with Lillian and Leah and Rebekah, and he was certain they would have been hard at work cleaning up the bloody mess that had been left in the kitchen.

Leah would never have left it, of that he was certain, and Naomi had shown herself to be at least as determined as Leah to keep a neat house. He chuckled again as he thought about it.

I am truly blessed.

FOUR

Rebekah looked out the window at the new layer of snow that had fallen overnight, covering the landscape.

Always more snow. Does it ever stop snowing here? When will I get the chance to get out of this haus and go somewhere... anywhere?

She stopped herself before her thoughts got carried away. She would just march herself downstairs and see what *Mamm* needed help with. There was always something to do.

Even though Caleb was healing well, he was not allowed to be on his leg at all, so he needed constant help. Of course, one of his *bruders* were always on hand in case he needed a helping hand to the bathroom, and they mostly took care of anything else he might need at the same time.

But with so many people in the *haus,* there was always something that needed doing. Certainly *Mamm* would have something for her to do, and keeping busy might help to take her mind off how lonely she was and how much she missed her home in Hope Springs.

It was especially difficult now since *Grossdaddi* and *Grossmammi* had gone back home. While they had been visiting, she had almost felt like home was here with her. But now they had returned to Hope Springs and Rebekah missed them so much.

And as much as she was trying to make the best of things, it was still difficult to think that she could ever truly fit in here.

The Fisher family was wonderful, to be sure, but they were nothing like what she was used to. There seemed to be something crazy that happened every day.

In the week since Caleb had been injured, Lillian had dropped a pot of *kaffe* and splashed it all over herself. It had been fresh off the stove top and she had some pretty nasty burns on her leg where it splashed under her skirt. Benjamin had sliced open his hand with a knife in the barn, though they were all thankful it was nothing like the cut on Caleb's leg. Leah had tripped over the rake that someone had neglected to put back in its proper place, leaving an impressive knot on her head. And little Matthew had fallen in the frozen creek that rushed along the back of the property.

If Elam hadn't been with him... well, she didn't want to think about what could have happened.

She didn't know how anyone kept from going positively crazy with so much going on at all hours of the day and night. And, as if the people didn't get into enough trouble, the animals got themselves into their fair share of messes as well.

One of Caleb's horses had gone into labor in the middle of the night and the whole *haus* had been a flurry of activity, everyone rushing this way or that and Caleb complaining that he could not get outside to help. Then one of the milk cows had gotten herself hung up in the fence beside the barn and had started bawling as if she were dying. Leah had assured Rebekah that it happened all the time and Bessie always bawled like that, but the whole thing had sounded pretty serious to Rebekah.

The whole place is a mad haus. That is for sure and for certain.

While it was true, she knew this was home now and she had to find a way to live with it all. She was simply not used to all of this activity. With eleven *bruders* and *schweschders*—never mind that the four eldest were married—they were here all the time, with children in tow. It was certain to be busier than anything Rebekah had ever known.

She stood and walked across the room, running a hand over her new bed that *Mamm* had covered with a familiar quilt from home. Even though *Grossmammi* had not entirely agreed with her *dochder's* decision to marry a man she hardly knew and move several states away, she had packed up their things and sent them to New York and Rebekah was grateful for it.

And I do not want to think of what would I do without anything to remind me of home.

She squared her shoulders, walked out of the room and headed down the hall, glancing in the small mirror as she went by to make sure her *kapp* was in place and no hair had escaped the tight bun underneath.

. . .

Leah watched her new *schweschder* as she walked into the kitchen, twisting her hands together in her apron as if she had something worrying on her mind. She wondered if it would be a *gut* time to approach Rebekah about spending some time together.

There was so much that she wanted to introduce

her new *schweschder* to. Everything Leah needed to do for the morning was long finished, with hours yet before she needed to get going on her afternoon chores.

As much as she would love to stay here and help Naomi with the baking, she felt oddly compelled to take Rebekah into town for a treat. Her new *schweschder* had been through so much change in the last two months, surely a trip into town for a treat would meet with her approval.

With that in mind, Leah sent her Rebekah a bright smile and walked over to where Naomi was kneading dough. She tried to infuse her voice with excitement, hoping that some of it might filter out to Rebekah as she listened to them talk.

"*Mamm,*" Leah closed her eyes for a moment. She loved the little thrill that rushed through her at the thought that she finally had a *Mamm* again and it was just as wonderful as she had always hoped. "Would it be okay if Rebekah and I go into town this morning?" She paused there a moment and waited until Naomi looked over at her with a slightly puzzled expression.

"I was thinking I could show her around a bit, maybe take her to some of the places I first took you when you asked me to show you around our town." She thought she could see a light of understanding in Naomi's eyes, but she went on for Rebekah's benefit.

"What with planning the wedding and all the snow, we haven't had much chance to show Rebekah our wonderful, little town. I'm finished with my morning chores and I really don't have anything else to do until this afternoon."

She paused another moment and then, just to make sure Naomi understood what she was getting at, she added.

"It would be such a *treat* to get out of the *haus* for a bit." And with the added emphasis she gave the word treat, Leah could see that Naomi understood exactly what she was trying to say, without her actually saying it.

"I think that is a wonderful *gut* idea. I would go with you but I have so much to do here." And Naomi winked at Leah as she said it. "You two will be allrecht by yourselves then?" Naomi left the question hanging, but Leah was already nodding her head and she didn't waste a moment.

Smiling widely, she rushed over, taking Rebekah by the hand and pulling her along to the back door. "It's a very *gut* thing you have already gotten dressed warmly. We're all ready to go." She kept up the chattering, telling Rebekah all about the town and the drive and the weather and how beautiful it was out today, not giving Rebekah a moment to argue.

. . .

Leah looked all around her at the beauty of the snow-covered fields and marveled at how clean and pristine the world looked when it snowed. It was wonderful to live in such a beautiful place as this. She wondered if the area Naomi and Rebekah had moved from was anything like their little hollow?

She turned her head to ask Rebekah and noticed a tear running down her cheek from the corner of her eye. Her head was turned toward the window and Leah wondered what could be making her new *schweschder* so sad. Was she missing home or just her grandparents. Was she upset over leaving behind her *freinden* or favorite places to explore?

Leah worried her lip just a bit as she tried to think of what she could say to her new *schweschder*. What would she want someone to say to her if their positions were reversed? What she had always missed was the things a mother would do and say—and she had that now.

Well, she told herself, *we will just have to find some new freinden for Rebekah—and I know some wunderbaar places to explore.* She would share them with Rebekah, who might eventually be comfortable enough to find more on her own.

She was thankful she had thought of this outing. Rebekah certainly did need a treat. And perhaps she also needed to get out of the *haus* a bit more. Maybe if she could see how wonderful the people were, she would begin to feel more at home here.

Leah looked around as they drove into town. There was no one nearby that she could introduce Rebekah to, but maybe there would be someone in *Sew Sweet*. And if not, maybe it would be enough to introduce her to Margaretta's delicious sticky buns.

She pulled up to the special parking area between *Sew Nice* and *Sew Sweet* and set the brake. Rebekah didn't move to get out; she sat there with her shoulders stiff, almost as if she were preparing to walk into the lion's den.

Leah stepped down out of the buggy and walked toward the front to tie up the team. Moments later, when she spotted Zeke Hershberger coming out of the mercantile down the street, suddenly she knew exactly what to do.

She had been trying for some time now to think of a way to let Zeke know that there was no chance for them to be more than *freinden*. She could never feel the same about him that he felt about her, but she hadn't been able to figure out how to let him know. Now that she was involved with Jacob Kurtz, it felt very wrong to continue to allow Zeke to think there could be anything between them.

But... maybe... if she could introduce Zeke to Rebekah, and if there was any interest between the two of them, it could solve both problems. Rebekah was such a beauty, Zeke would be blind not to see it. And perhaps Zeke's charm and sly wit could help Rebekah get over at least some of her home-sickness.

"Zeke. You have to come and meet Rebekah." She waved to him as she called out. He saw her immediately and a smile spread across his handsome face.

Oh I hope this works.

"Leah, I didn't know you would be in town today. Did you have any trouble on the roads?" His smile had been replaced by a look of concern and Leah couldn't help but feeling that he should be able to see that he clearly felt more like a *bruder* to her.

He certainly acts like one.

"*Danki,* Zeke for asking. *Nee,* I had no trouble and I didn't know I would be coming into town today. It was a very unexpected decision." As she said it, she moved around to Rebekah's side of the buggy and she could see out of the corner of her eye that Rebekah was looking through the small side window with more interest than she'd shown for anything else since arriving here.

That's surely a gut sign, Leah told herself, opening the door and holding out her hand with a bit of a flourish.

"This is my new *schweschder,* Rebekah. You know her *Mamm* married my *Dat* a month ago." Leah was encouraged by the fact that Zeke had not taken his eyes off Rebekah's since he had looked up at her. In fact, they were both looking at each other and they gave no indication they were likely to look anywhere else anytime soon.

"With all the snow, we haven't exactly had time to get around to meet everyone." Leah stopped speaking because it was clear neither one of them was listening to her. She nearly rubbed her hands together in delight. This was working so much better than she had expected.

"Zeke," Leah tapped him on the shoulder to get his attention. She even had to wait a few seconds before he replied with a vague "...hmm?"

"We were going to get a treat at *Sew Sweet.* Would you be interested in joining us?" Leah had barely gotten the words out before Rebekah joined in.

"Oh yes, you must. We should all get in out of the cold."

Before Rebekah even finished speaking, Zeke was nodding—and he stepped forward to hold out a hand to help Rebekah out of the buggy, still looking into her eyes.

. . .

Rebekah looked down at the young man holding out a hand to her. She felt a warmth start at her cheeks and spread through her whole body. She certainly had not seen this coming. Only a minute ago she'd been feeling so home-sick she didn't know how she would be able to stand it.

Now she was feeling like she had come home... not to her previous home or even the home she and her mother had moved into with Samuel and his family. No, this was a feeling of a home she had been unknowingly searching for. She felt warmth and excitement and something she couldn't put a name to, but it was a *gut* thing—a very *gut* thing—of this she was certain. Suddenly she was glad she hadn't made up an excuse to stay home when Leah suggested they come into town. She almost had, and she mentally kicked herself, thinking of it now. She would have missed this—and she was for sure glad she hadn't missed this.

She stepped down carefully, leaning on Zeke's

strength as he guided her. When her feet were on the ground, she looked up and up and up and finally met Zeke's eyes.

My, but he's a tall one, she thought as she continued to hold onto his hand while he helped her up over the icy curb. When all three of them stood on the sidewalk, Rebekah finally managed to look away from Zeke and over at Leah, who was looking at the two of them with a big smile on her face.

Why... she planned this.

Rebekah knew she should be bothered that Leah had maneuvered her, she couldn't find any irritation toward her new *schweschder*. In fact, she was grateful. All this time she had been worrying that Leah might have a claim to this young man. Well, that was clearly not the case. If anything, Leah was pushing the two of them together, which suited Rebekah just fine. She returned Leah's smile and then looked over to the shops next to them.

"Did you say something about a treat?"

"I did. *Jah. Sew Sweet* has some of the best baked goods around. I thought it would be a *gut* place to start." Leah motioned to the shop right next to them

"What do you think?" She looked at Rebekah and then at Zeke. Zeke looked at Rebekah before answering.

"They have wonderful hot cocoa. It would be a *gut*

way to warm up on such a cold day." Zeke told her. Rebekah nodded, although she wasn't really feeling cold anymore. Then she looked to Leah, who was nodding, so she turned to walk toward the door.

They hadn't take two steps when Rebekah felt her foot slide on a patch of ice and a startled scream rushed up her throat. Before it could escape, strong arms caught her and lifted her over the patch of ice and onto solid ground again.

She looked up at Zeke and felt the breath catch in her throat. They stood there for what felt like a very long time before she was finally able to manage a breathless "thank you."

"You are welcome." Then he took her hand, tucked it firmly around his crooked elbow and turned to follow Leah, who was standing at the door with one hand on the knob and the other pressed to her heart.

The look of surprise on her face was quickly turning back to a smile though. In fact, when Rebekah looked at her, Leah ducked her head and Rebekah heard what sounded suspiciously like a giggle.

Rebekah was not a bit surprised to realize she felt a smile tugging at the corners of her own mouth as well. She was almost astonished to realize it didn't matter one bit to her whether Leah was laughing at her clumsiness or because of how perfectly her plan was working. Indeed, Rebekah was far too happy to let either idea bother her.

When she looked up at Zeke again, it seemed as if he was enjoying himself as well. His smile was spread across his face and he was holding a firm hand over her own while watching where they were walking as they moved slowly toward the door Leah held ready to open. For the first time in what felt like forever, Rebekah began to think like she just might fit very well... right where she was.

As the new feeling of contentment washed over her, she felt a tremendous weight lift off of her. It felt as if she was walking on air instead of hard-packed snow.

When they reached the door, Leah swept in ahead of them, holding the door open long enough for Zeke to catch it and hold it open for the two of them. The moment she walked through the doorway, Rebekah could see why Leah wanted to bring her here.

Aside from the heavenly smells everywhere, it seemed as if this was the place to gather in town. At least half the people in the room were plain folk but there were conversations all over between plain and *Englisch.*

Rebekah was startled to see such a thing. Back in Hope Springs, they had occasionally done business with the *Englisch,* but no one had been encouraged to make *freinden* with them. Clearly that was not the case here.

This might take some getting used to.

Zeke headed for the large glass-topped counter that ran nearly the length of one wall. Leah was already standing there chatting with an *Englischer* woman with golden-toned skin and midnight black hair who was standing behind the large counter.

As they moved toward the counter, Leah motioned them to come over to where she stood. When Rebekah got closer to the two of them, she felt puzzled. The woman had a youthful face, but her eyes told a different story.

There was a world of knowledge in those eyes. That must be why it was so difficult to determine her age. She was obviously someone who had seen more than her fair share of life's troubles.

"Margaretta, this is who I've been telling you about."

Rebekah felt her cheeks warm at the thought that Leah had been discussing her with someone she didn't know.

"My new *schweschder,* Rebekah."

Those words, however, made any embarrassment Rebekah felt quickly disappear as the warmth from her cheeks traveled down and settled in her heart. She had yet to hear Leah refer to her as a *schweschder* and she had to admit to herself that it was nice. She looked over at Leah, who was smiling even wider than she had been only a moment ago and then back up at Zeke, who was smiling down at her. Suddenly she felt better about moving here than she had the whole time since she had arrived.

She looked back over at Margaretta and realized she was holding out a hand. Rebekah took her hand from Zeke's arm and shook the offered hand, finding a surprisingly firm grip from such tiny fingers.

"I'm pleased to meet you, Rebekah. I've heard so much about you from this one. It's great to finally get the chance to meet you and see if you live up to the advance publicity."

Rebekah felt her mouth drop open in surprise. It took a moment, but she managed to shut it again while she tried to think of something to say in return. It was several moments before she realized that Margaretta was teasing her. There was a twinkle of mischief in her eyes and she was already giggling.

"I'm sorry. I couldn't resist. Leah said you were very serious and as you can tell, I'm not." Rebekah noticed out of the corner of her eye that Leah was nodding her head vigorously as Margaretta spoke.

"Margaretta has had fun at my expense many times." Leah smiled as she said it. Rebekah hoped that meant she was happy to be introducing them and not that she was enjoying Margaretta's teasing.

Margaretta was nodding as she giggled again. "Oh, *jah*. We have a lot of fun with each other." She nudged Leah and then they were both giggling, as if they were enjoying a private joke at each other's expense.

Rebekah found herself wondering if Margaretta realized she had used the Pennsylvania Dutch version of what she'd just said. Either she did and that was the joke, or she didn't and it was just a slip. Perhaps it was because she heard so many of her customers using it, but before she could say anything, Margaretta went on.

"It took Leah a while to get used to my sense of humor though, didn't it, girl?"

"Oh, *jah*, it did." Leah was giggling and nodding as she sad it.

The four of them stood like that until Leah's and Margaretta's laughter finally began to slow.

"Okay. Time to get serious. Wouldn't want the boss to dock me." Margaretta winked at Rebekah as she said it. That was surprising, to say the least. Rebekah didn't think anyone had ever winked at her before. She had seen people do it, but never had a wink been directed at her.

Today is just a day of firsts it seems. I wonder what else I will discover while I am here.

The thought was oddly comforting. These people were not treating her like an outsider. They were treating her like one of their own, which was comforting. There were just so many things she would have to get used to... or so it seemed.

FIVE

Naomi looked up from the letter in her hands as the door to the mudroom opened and quickly shut. She waited, trying to decide if she should call out and see who had come in or if she could figure it out.

It didn't take more than a moment to realize it must be Leah and Rebekah since she was hearing feminine giggles and the stomping of tiny feet. She smiled at the sounds of laughter coming from both *maedels*. Leah's idea had been a *gut* one. This was what she had been wanting for Rebekah all along.

Leah was such a *gut maedel*. Naomi felt doubly blessed to have two such wonderful *dochdern* to call her own. And now that they were *freinden,* perhaps

Rebekah would stop being so home-sick and begin to feel like a part of this family.

"*Mamm, we*'re back."

Naomi felt a little thrill rush through her when she realized it was Leah's voice calling out to her. It was not the first time Leah had referred to her with such familiarity, but the wonder in it had yet to wear off for Naomi.

"I'm in the kitchen." She called out in response and a moment later, she could hear stockinged feet padding across the mudroom floor, accompanied by more giggles.

Naomi was looking at the opening that connected the two rooms when Leah and Rebekah practically tumbled through it, holding onto each other and laughing loudly now.

Naomi felt laughter bubbling up within her at the beautiful sight. She let out a couple of small giggles. It was so *gut* to hear her two *dochders* getting along like they had always been *schweschders*.

They were laughing and talking in little half sentences as they rushed into the room, their stockings slipping a little on the smooth wood floor. Naomi sat there watching them, smiling as they came over to the table and dropped into chairs on the opposite side, fairly gasping for breath.

"I suppose that means you had a *gut* time." Her words set off another bout of breathless giggles. She looked over at Leah and raised one eyebrow in a question she hoped Leah would understand.

Her daughter nodded her head. then laughed and weakly waved a hand in the air, which Naomi took to mean they would talk about it later.

"So," She paused and waited until the giggles slowed a little. "What have you two been up to?"

It was still nearly a minute before they managed to stop laughing. It was a *gut* sign, but Naomi was more than a little curious to know what had them in such a fit of laughter.

"*Mamm*, you met Leah's friend, Margaretta. J*ah*? Rebekah managed to get out finally.

Naomi was nodding and a smile spread over her face as soon as she heard the name Margaretta. It was beginning to make sense now. Margaretta had a somewhat odd sense of humor. The girls must have been enjoying a lovely, silly time with her in town then.

"We met today when Leah took me into town and we stopped in at *Sew Sweet* for a treat." Rebekah laughed again as she said it.

Naomi thought back to the first time she had met the young woman. Margaretta was a young woman who knew how to craft a joke, to be sure.

Margaretta had managed to get Leah laughing that day as well. Naomi knew Leah had been in a very fowl temper when she had shown up at their *haus* unannounced.

She had been polite and hospitable though and had only begun to loosen up when Margaretta started in with her silliness, which meant that Margaretta was now one of Naomi's favorite people in Windy Gap.

She was glad to hear that Rebekah liked her as well. She might not know well all that Rebekah had dealt with in Hope Springs, but she knew that her *dochder* had not been out with *freinden* much.

Rebekah had attended the singings, but only because her *Grossmammi* had insisted. Naomi had tried to tell her *Mamm* that it was not a *gut* idea to make Rebekah go, but *Mamm* had insisted that Rebekah was a young *maedel* and she needed to be with the other young people whenever she could.

Naomi had always wondered if that had added to Rebekah's unhappiness, because she seemed to dread the youth gatherings. It was the closest she had ever come to being disrespectful to her *Grossmammi*.

Now they were here and Rebekah had a fresh chance to make *freinden,* and with Leah's help, too.

"Is that a letter from *Grossmammi, Mamm*? Did it come in today's mail?"

"Jah, I have been expecting a letter for several days, but what I wasn't expecting to hear is that your *Grossmammi* is still upset about our move to Windy Gap."

"But why, Mamm? I don't understand. When I was staying with them, *Grossmammi* seemed fine with the idea of you marrying Samuel."

"Well *dochder*, your grandparents miss us, especially you. They say it's very lonely—and quiet—and they don't like it one bit." She looked at Rebekah and then at Leah, distressed to bring down their happy mood, even a little.

"We should tell them to move here!" Rebekah said, startling Naomi in her exuberance.

"*Jah*, we should do that." Leah added. "*Mamm*, your *bruders* live in Lancaster, *jah*? New York is much closer to Lancaster than Ohio, *ain't so*?"

"Actually they are closer to Hershey, but *jah*, it would be much closer." Naomi answered somewhat absently as she looked back and forth between the two *maedels*. They were not *bedauerlich* at all. Instead they were both *eiferich*. They sat, looking hopefully at Naomi. As she thought about what they were suggesting, she realized it could solve the problem. It was a *gut* idea.

Mamm had been saying for years that she wished

they could be closer to her *bruders* and their families. This would certainly give them that chance. They would be closer to everyone. Living here would give them more time with Naomi; time they had missed out on while she had been caring for John.

"We have a wonderful *gut Daddi haus*." Leah was nearly bouncing out of her seat. "It's the *haus* that was on the land when *Dat* bought it. He wanted a big family so he built a much bigger *haus* for us, but there was not a thing wrong with that one so he left it there."

"But what sort of shape is it in, Leah?" Naomi tucked her bottom lip between her teeth and worried it a bit while she waited for Leah's answer.

"There may be some cleaning to do, but we have kept it in *gut* order, just in case it was ever needed." Her smile was so wide, Naomi did not think it could get any bigger, and her excitement was contagious.

She could feel herself warming to the idea. *Mamm* and *Dat* here, with them all the time. It would be like it had been in Hope Springs but even better, because she was no longer tied to home as she had once been.

"The decision will be theirs, but..." she watched Leah's smile slip just a little before she brightened again.

"We will pray. *Gotte* will show us what is the right thing to do. If it is His *wille*, they will *kumme*." Rebekah was nodding her head now, too. They both looked so *eiferich,* Naomi could feel excitement blooming deep within her as well.

"We will write to them right away and ask them to consider it." She turned to get up, then sat back down again.

"We should make sure it is allrecht with Samuel first." She stopped a moment before continuing. She was not used to this. It had been a long time since she had needed to check with someone else. Instead of being bothersome, she found she liked the feeling of having someone else to share the decisions with. It was a comfort, to be sure.

"He will be fine with it. I know he will. He has been saying it is a shame for such a beautiful *haus* to just sit there, unused." Leah was nodding her head and bouncing again and Rebekah joined her after only a few seconds.

"Let's go ask him, schweschder." Both *maedels* jumped up from their chairs and rushed to the back door to put their boots back on, talking all the time about how they would ask *Dat* and what fun they would have showing *Grossdaddi* and *Grossmammi* the area.

Naomi laughed a moment later at the sound of their boots rushing across the back porch. She hoped they didn't slip on the way to the barn in their excitement.

Oh well. If they do, they'll catch each other... or land together on the icy ground.

She looked through *Mamm's* letter one more time before getting up to check on the pie she had put in the oven an hour ago.

. . .

Rebekah looked over at Leah as they walked arm in arm toward the barn. She had enjoyed spending time with Leah in town and now that they were back at home, she was beginning to see all that she had been missing out on.

The farm even looked different to her. She looked out over the fields and for the first time, she could see the beauty there. Yes, there was more snow than she was used to, but she could see more clearly why Leah loved it.

It gave everything a clean, fresh look. It was almost like someone had thrown a white covering over the land, giving it a snug cozy look, even though it was exceptionally cold.

Rebekah was thrilled to realize they would not be stuck inside with so much snow everywhere. The main roads were mostly clear and their buggy wheels were somehow designed to work perfectly in the snow. She would have to ask Samuel about that sometime.

"This is such a *gut* idea, don't you think?" Leah said suddenly, distracting Rebekah from her thoughts.

Rebekah was surprised to hear uncertainty in Leah's voice. Here she had thought Leah was *so* confident and *gelassenheit* all of the time. Strange to think she had actually been intimidated by how perfect her new *schweschder* was.

She was beginning to see that her impression had been wrong. Yes, Leah was an exceptional young *maedel,* but she was certainly no more perfect than Rebekah herself. And clearly she harbored some of the same insecurities that plagued Rebekah as well. Otherwise, what reason would Leah have to be worried over her *Dat's* answer?

"I think it is a very *gut* idea and I am very glad you thought of it." Rebekah patted Leah's arm where it was linked through her own, before turning back toward the barn.

She felt Leah's arm relax and realized she had not even noticed how tense her new *schweschder* had been before. She had most certainly misjudged Leah.

"You know what else..." Rebekah asked with a hesitant smile.

"What?" Leah asked.

"I think *Grossdaddi* and *Grossmammi* will want to

kumme."

Leah's breath came out in a little puff of laughter. She stopped as her feet slid on a large, icy patch on the ground the same time as she felt her schweschder began to wobble.

"Careful!" Rebekah shouted, though she could see that Leah was being careful as they lost control.

They slipped and slid and their feet nearly came out from under them. Rebekah took hold of Leah. Leah's hands were grasping at Rebekah's as they slid around on the large patch of ice. By the time they got their footing, they were both laughing.

Quickly and as carefully as possible, they moved off the icy patch of ground. Rebekah leaned over, resting her hands on her knees in an attempt to catch her breath. Leah went even further and plopped right down on the snow-covered ground beside the path.

"Well, that was something." Leah said with another laugh. Rebekah was nodding her head as she joined in. "Imagine if we had been wearing skates. It would have been quite a sight."

"Oh! That reminds me. I have been meaning to suggest a skating party." Leah was pulling herself up already and she took both of Rebekah's hands in hers. "Oh, this will be fun!" Leah was nearly yelling as she again pulled Rebekah toward the barn.

SIX

Rebekah lay under the covers, looking up at the ceiling, trying to stay still as she listened to the small clock beside her bed tick out the minutes. How long should she wait until she moved?

Ach! How long will it take Leah to go to sleep? I cannot stay here all nacht; I will miss Zeke. And I cannot fall asleep. He will not be making any noise and he will not wait long.

This she knew from experience. The one time a young man had shown a flashlight into her window, the light had woken her, but she had stayed in bed a little too long. By the time curiosity had gotten the better of her, she had looked out the window to see him riding away in his buggy.

The next gathering he had *kumme* with Amy Muller. No other young man had tried since.

I will not miss this chance with Zeke.

Rebekah thought she heard the large clock downstairs strike the hour and she nearly jumped out of bed when she saw a tiny beam of light *kumme* through the window glass.

At the same time that Rebekah's feet hit the cold floor, Leah threw back the covers. When she looked up and saw Rebekah, a small smile appeared on her face.

"Ah... Rebekah, I didn't mean to wake you." Leah said, with a strange sound in her voice.

Rebekah thought a moment before she said anything. Could Leah possibly have been waiting for the same thing she had been?

"You did not wake me, Leah." She looked at Leah as another beam flashed through the window. The memory of David Stoltzfus made her move quickly to stand.

I knew it, Rebekah thought as she moved toward the window. *She is expecting someone, too. Ach! Could it be the same person I was hoping for?* Rebekah was distracted thinking about who it might be.

She didn't have to wait long to know the answer. The moment she reached the window, she could see who was waiting. She had to stifle a gasp when she saw who stood on the snowy ground below the window.

Her cousin Jacob had a companionable arm slung over Zeke's shoulder as they stood there together, waiting for the *maedels*. Rebekah looked over at Leah and they burst into laughter. As quickly as the sounds escaped, they each clamped a hand over their mouth to stop the laughter so no one else in the *haus* would hear them.

Waving down to the boys, Rebekah turned back to Leah, who was standing there with a big smile on her face.

"Looks like we both have a secret." She whispered the words, but Rebekah could hear nothing in her tone but amusement.

They giggled at the same time and then they were both scrambling to their feet. Leah waved out the window until Jacob nodded. When he did, Rebekah saw that Leah was holding up both hands. She must be telling him they would be out in ten minutes.

She looked down at herself. She hadn't actually gotten undressed. She had just slipped under the covers when Leah wasn't paying attention.

Should I wait for Leah, she wondered, and immediately realized what a silly question that was.

Of course she would wait. Leah would not take the

entire ten minutes. She looked to be just as much in a hurry as Rebekah was.

"I didn't realize you had not gotten undressed. Why didn't I think of that?" Leah whispered to Rebekah.

"Probably because you didn't want me to be suspicious." Rebekah let out a small laugh with her words, but quickly smothered it. "I won't go down until you do anyway. Don't get in a hurry on my account," she told her new *schweschder*.

She started to ask Leah how often she did this, but the words didn't make it past her lips. She just stood there, watching Leah as she pinned herself together and pulled her hair back into her *kapp*.

I should be more grateful than I have been. If not for Leah, I might never have even met Zeke.

And she knew it was true. In fact, if she'd had her way, she would not have even seen him the morning they had dropped off her grandparents at the train station. She would have been visiting with her *Aenti* and *Onkel*.

And now she had Leah to thank for introducing them.

It is a wonderful gut blessing to have a schweschder.

She made a point then, of offering up thanks to *Gotte* as well. This had all been in His plans and she must remember that His plans were so much better than her own could ever be.

"Rebekah, are you ready?" Leah whispered, and Rebekah nodded.

Together, they carefully crept out of their room and down the hall. As they went down the stairs, Leah pointed down and motioned to her. Rebekah remembered that one of the steps made noise. From Leah's gestures, Rebekah figured out that she needed to skip the one that Leah did.

When they were almost to the bottom, Leah stepped delicately over one of the steps and Rebekah followed; careful to place her foot securely on the next step.

In the mudroom, they pulled on their boots and slipped into their coats. When Rebekah reached for the back door, Leah closed a hand over hers and shook her head slightly when Rebekah looked up at her.

The door must make a lot of noise, too. Quickly, she let go of the door and motioned for Leah to go first.

She breathed a sigh of relief that Leah was with her. If Leah had not *kumme* with her, she might have already woken someone up with the noisy step or this door. She watched as Leah opened the door very slowly and then slipped through the tiny space.

Thankful for the small build she had inherited from *Mamm,* Rebekah slipped through after Leah and was surprised to find both boys had moved to the edge of the porch to stand together.

Leah walked over to the edge next to Jacob and looked down at him with such *lieb,* there was no doubt to the depth of their feelings. Rebekah felt heat rush to her cheeks.

They look so happy, she thought to herself. She was *eiferich* for her cousin—and for her new *schweschder,* as well—but she was not accustomed to seeing such strength of emotion.

As she turned away, she noticed that Zeke was watching her. He looked up at her as she stood there on the porch. After a moment, he reached up to her with both hands. She had not been prepared for him to lift her down, but it seemed the *schmaert* thing to do, so she leaned forward until his hands were around her waist, and then he was swinging her down to the ground.

The heat from her cheeks had spread to where his hands touched her waist and everywhere her body was pushed up against his. When he set her down, she even worried for a moment that her trembling knees might not hold her, but he held onto her, looking into her eyes until she heard someone clear their throat noisily behind them.

Zeke only chuckled and then a grin spread across his face that she had not seen before. It looked more than a little mischievous and she could feel a strange fluttering feeling in her stomach as she looked up at him.

"*Kumme* on, Zeke," Jacob whispered "We have plenty of time for that later."

Zeke took her hand then and pulled her along with them as they made their way along the edge of the driveway toward the waiting buggies.

"I was thinking," Zeke began, and everyone turned to look at him. "There is a *wunderbaar kaffe* shop just outside town. They are open late on Friday *nacht*." he stopped a moment and then went on when no one else said anything. "It would be much warmer than just riding along the back roads."

Jacob and Leah looked at each other for several moments before Jacob looked back at Zeke. "*Jah*, that sounds *gut* to me."

Then Leah spoke up, "What about you, Rebekah?" and Rebekah could only nod her head in Leah's direction, thankful for the bright moon. Otherwise Leah could never have seen her nod.

Leah nodded back and then she and Jacob took off down the side of the gravel drive.

Rebekah breathed another sigh of relief as she followed Zeke along the same path. She certainly did not want to tell her new *schweschder,* or Zeke for that matter, that she had secretly been terrified of being all alone with him. Since she had never experienced what went on when two young people went out late courting, she had worried that she would do something terribly embarrassing. She was very glad he had mentioned the *kaffe* shop.

At the end of the drive, they went to their separate buggies and Zeke again placed his hands on Rebekah's waist, this time to lift her up into the buggy.

She tried to force her thoughts away from the feel of his hands about her waist, but all she could seem to think about was the strength in those hands and in his arms. He swung her up onto the buggy seat as if she were light as a feather, though he was as gentle with her as he would have been with a delicate piece of glass.

As she settled herself on the bench, he reached into the back area of the buggy. A moment later, he draped a thick, warm blanket over her lap. She could not help wondering how he had kept the blanket so warm, but the answer was obvious when he lifted another thick blanket and then placed it at her feet.

He must have several hot bricks wrapped up in it.

The thought warmed her even more so than the blankets. Even though he had clearly been thinking of her comfort, he had also made a suggestion that they go somewhere indoors so that they would not have to sit out in the cold.

"Are you warm enough?" She jumped a little at the sound of his voice so close beside her. She nodded her head, and then after a minute decided that she needed to say something to him about his thoughtfulness.

However, the words that came out were not at all what she had intended to say, "Why did you suggest the *kaffe* shop if you already had the bricks and the blankets?" Once the words had left her mouth, she felt like she had stuffed both feet in behind them.

Zeke surprised her by laughing. She looked over at him and it wasn't hard to tell that he was not laughing at her, but it still didn't make her feel all that much better.

"I suggested the *kaffe* shop because it is much colder out tonight than I expected. And I thought it might be nice for us to all sit together and talk a bit." he looked over at her as he spoke. "I don't know about you, but I was more than a little surprised when I arrived and found Jacob Kurtz outside your window."

"He's my cousin." Rebekah said, probably a little too quickly, because Zeke chuckled again before answering.

"I know that... now."

Rebekah sat there thinking about that. She'd had no

idea about Jacob and Leah. Why had neither of them said anything to her about their relationship?

Like you told her about Zeke? A little voice inside her head reminded her. Rebekah cringed at the truth of it.

Ach! Fine! So I didn't tell Leah about Zeke. She sat there, arguing with herself and failed to notice that Zeke was still speaking to her.

"Rebekah, *was iss letz?*"

And even though she heard him, she couldn't come up with anything to say. She let her head drop heavily into her hands and she just shook her head back and forth.

After a few minutes, she realized they weren't moving, and she looked up. Zeke was sitting there, just looking at her.

What am I supposed to do now? She thought.

"Rebekah," Zeke said again, taking her hands in his. *"Was iss letz?"*

And then the words came. They poured out of her and she couldn't seem to stop. "Everything is just so weird. Nothing in my life has been normal... not ever. And now I'm here and I miss my grandparents and I hardly know anyone and I... I don't know. I should be happy. I know I should. Leah has been so wonderful to me and now there's you..."

She waved a hand at him, as if that should explain everything. "I do not know what is wrong with me. I just don't know..." and the last word came out more of a wail.

She stopped and dropped her head back down but since he held her hands, she just sat there as she waited for him to say something. He sat there, holding her hands and looking at her as if he didn't know what to say—or do.

"I'm sorry. I don't mean to dump all of this on you." she looked down at the floor of the buggy, feeling the flames of embarrassment on her cheeks. He would likely never be shining a light in her window again.

"Rebekah," he squeezed her hands lightly to get her attention. "It sounds as if you have been through so much in your young life."

She looked up at that, shocked that he did not sound at all upset or angry with her.

"*Danki* for sharing all of that with me."

At that, she was speechless. He was actually thanking her for dumping all of her worries and troubles on him?

He looked down at their feet, but then he looked back up at her, shyly, "Though I do hope that you can find something here to make your days happier. Perhaps even someone..." and the look in his eyes was all she needed to abandon her worries about what was proper. Without another thought, she threw her arms around him.

"*Danki*, Zeke. You do not know what that means to me," she said against the thick, soft wool of his coat.

They sat there like that for several minutes before Zeke pulled away gently. "Let's get indoors, shall we?" and he turned back to the horses.

In another minute, they were back on the road and heading toward town. Rebekah sat there, trying to look at him out of the corner of her eyes.

"Did you and Leah ever..." and Rebekah clamped a hand over her mouth. Once again she had said something she had not meant to.

Ach! What is wrong with me!

She knew the answer to that question though. Zeke Hershberger did something to her brain.

She looked over at him because he was laughing again.

"I am not laughing at you, Rebekah Yoder."

How does he always know just what I am thinking?

"This certainly is a *nacht* for confessions." He rubbed a hand over his face before continuing. "*Jah*, I once thought there was something between Leah and me." He looked over at her before he said the next words. "It only took one look at your face to know that whatever I may have felt for Leah was more like a *bruder* feels for his *schweschder.*" Something about the look in his eyes made the heat rush back into Rebekah's cheeks.

She couldn't seem to look away from his eyes after that. Something passed between them as they looked at each other for what felt like a century, but could only have been a few seconds, before Zeke finally turned his head to look back at the road.

When he looked away, Rebekah placed a hand to her chest. Her heart was galloping faster than any of *Grossdaddi's* horses ever had, and her breaths were coming in short, little gasps.

She tried to tell herself that it had something to do with the cold, but she knew otherwise. Something very serious had just happened Something she had never truthfully expected, and certainly not in Windy Gap. She had just lost her heart to Zeke Hershberger.

The thought should have frightened her. After all, she barely knew this young man. But the thought did not frighten her at all. She even slid a little closer to him on the bench as they drove through the snow that had begun to fall.

SEVEN

When they drove into town, Rebekah was surprised to see so many vehicles on the road or parked in the spaces lining the street.

Shouldn't people be at home on such a cold nacht?

As they drove past *Sew Nice* and *Sew Sweet,* Rebekah shook her head a little at the curious names. She would have to ask Leah about that. There had to be a story there.

They kept going until Rebekah could see that they were nearly to the edge of town. They actually drove past the building, which sat on a small hill and was called—oddly enough—*Higher Grounds.* Rebekah shook her head again as she thought about it.

People here have too much time on their hands, I think.

Just beyond the building, there was a roped off area with several long hitching posts. This was where Zeke steered them. When they pulled in to the gravel lot, she could see Jacob's courting buggy. It looked as if he had just parked as well.

Had they stopped off somewhere, too? She blushed again as she realized why they perhaps would have stopped somewhere. Would Leah and Jacob think that she Zeke had been up to the same thing?

Well they certainly will if they notice my pink cheeks, she told herself as she laid a hand on either cheek, hoping to cool them just a bit.

The buggy rocked a little when Zeke hopped down and then settled as he walked around to where Rebekah was waiting. She turned to help him as he reached up to her.

The moment his hands touched her waist, even though she knew she couldn't possibly feel his touch through her dress and long coat, warmth spread across her middle.

She struggled not to blush, but as he lifted her down, his eyes met hers and every coherent thought in her head scrambled at the look she could see there. Clearly he knew what she was thinking, and unless she was much mistaken, he was thinking very much the same thing.

"Are you two ready?" Rebekah heard Jacob call out to them, and she was relieved when Zeke answered.

"Go ahead in; get us a table. We'll be there soon." she heard Jacob's answering chuckle and Leah's giggle but she couldn't seem to take her eyes off of Zeke's face.

Suddenly Zeke looked very serious, which worried Rebekah. She wanted to ask him what was going on, but the words wouldn't *kumme*.

"Rebekah, there is something I must tell you now. I had thought it could wait until the next time we see each other, but I am thinking now that it can't."

A part of her wanted to panic at his words, except that he had mentioned the next time they saw each other. If he was about to tell her he had changed his mind about her, he wouldn't be talking about a next time... *would he?*

"Rebekah, I have watched so many of my *gut freinden* court young *maedels* and they all seem to see nothing wrong with rushing into the..." he stopped a moment and he looked so uncomfortable, she couldn't help wondering what he was about to divulge. *How bad could it be?*

"There's no use delaying. I'm sorry Rebekah, it's

just... so many of my *freinden* have given me such a hard time over this. They all think I am being *gegisch,* but I cannot help how I feel. I want things to be special for my, well, for my..." he waved a hand weakly in the air beside them

Then he alarmed her by turning away from her. She put a hand on his shoulder and squeezed lightly. He was such a *gut* young man. She could not imagine anything so terrible that he could not even face her, but she was determined that nothing he said would make her turn away from him.

"What is it, Zeke?" She moved her hand as his shoulders moved, and it appeared he was bracing himself before turning to her.

"I have made a vow that I will not kiss anyone until my wedding day." He let out a tremendous breath with the words, almost as if he had been holding his breath and it had fairly exploded with the expulsion of his words.

She took a moment to think about what he had just said. What was so bad about not wanting to kiss someone before you were married to them? It seemed a very *gut* idea to her. This was the news he had been afraid to share with her? *Truly?*

She put her hand back on his shoulder and waited until he looked at her. "Zeke, I don't understand. Why would that be a bad thing? It sounds very *schmaert* to me."

She was captivated with the look that came into his eyes. It was not the same as the one before. This was not an excited, heated look. It was extremely tender and there was something in his eyes that she had not seen before.

However, before she could even try to figure it out, her cousin stepped out and called to them.

Zeke smiled as he took her hand and pulled her to the *kaffe haus,* following Jacob back through the door.

Her cousin was busily muttering something under his breath as he walked back into the *kaffe haus.* She couldn't understand most of what he said, but she thought she picked out something about "sparking on their own time" and she laughed a little as she thought of the conversation she and Zeke had just finished.

Zeke turned to look at her and his grin was spread across his face. Clearly he, too, was enjoying what Jacob was complaining about.

She allowed him to pull her along and even chuckled a little at the irony that Jacob clearly thought she and Zeke had been sitting in the buggy doing the very thing Zeke had just told her they would not be doing.

Wait! Does that mean he doesn't plan to ever kiss

me? Or, is he telling me this because he wants me to be the one he will finally kiss and he wants me to know now so that I'm not surprised when he moves quickly?

Her thoughts were confusing and more than a little scrambled as she followed Jacob and Zeke through the dim *kaffe haus*. She could see several people sitting at tables with books and laptops spread out around them, but in the darker corners, there were mostly couples, even one or two who were not so young.

Everyone was being respectful though; even the couples that were sitting very close together. As they moved further into the large room, she could see a few of the couple's lips met more than once but they were not making a spectacle of themselves and she was grateful for it.

When Jacob finally stopped in front of a table where Leah sat waiting, Rebekah took a moment to look all around the room. It really was a nice place. The room was broken up in an unusual design, using several half walls, with seating scattered all over in little groupings. There was also a large number of tables tucked away in corners.

Only a few feet from where they stood, there was a long counter with a large glassed-in display running at least half the length of it. Beside the glass display, there was an old-fashioned cash register and a large empty space of counter.

On the long counter against the back wall, there was a monstrous brass machine that looked completely foreign to her. There were several large glass tubes full of coffee beans that flanked the large, brass machine and several other odd-looking machines that were placed across the long, wood space.

Otherwise, the décor was fairly simple. The walls were wood and brick, covered by what looked like pencil sketches in varying shapes and sizes. Each picture was framed, using a simple design, in smooth, dark wood and hung on a brick section of wall.

When Zeke moved toward the long counter, she followed him. Not just because he still held her hand firmly, either. She was very curious about this *kaffe* shop. There had been a coffee shop in the nearby town of Hope Springs, back in Ohio, but it had been part of a popular chain. She had not spent much time inside due to the loud music blasting from speakers that must have been hidden everywhere, and there was an overpowering smell of incense.

There was little or no resemblance in this delightful haven, filled with only the quiet music of many soft voices and *gut* smells of *kaffe* and baked goods.

When Zeke stepped up to the counter, she looked up at the large board hanging over the back counter, with the menu written out artfully in chalk across it. There were so many choices; how did anyone ever choose?

She looked over at Zeke and tried to tell him with her eyes that she had no idea what to order. He smiled at her and squeezed her hand, before turning back to place their order.

Rebekah looked at the young woman who stepped up behind the counter. She was dressed modestly, but nothing about her clothing was plain. Her sweater looked as if it was hand-knit, but it was a riot of colors and wild patterns. And her skirt nearly touched the floor, but it was made up of varying panels that should not have gone together, but somehow seemed to.

Still, there was something about her... She had a way about her that reminded Rebekah of her own *Mamm* and she was soft-spoken as she repeated Zeke's order back to him.

As she turned to prepare their drinks, Rebekah could see that she wore her hair long, and it hung down her back in a tangle of curls, tied back from her face with what looked like a handkerchief.

"What did you order for me?" Rebekah whispered to Zeke.

"Hot cocoa." I don't know how you like your *kaffe,* but Miranda makes hers very strong so I thought cocoa would be a better choice for you. Unless you would prefer *kaffe*..." and Rebekah felt the heat fill her again, settling in the general area of her heart.

He is just so wonderful.

Lieb settled like a warm blanket around her.

"*Danki*, Zeke. That is so thoughtful. I do prefer hot cocoa." Suddenly embarrassed, she looked over to where they had left Leah and Jacob. The two of them were sitting with their heads close together and they were talking in low tones.

There was something about the way the two of them were looking at each other... it was the first time Rebekah really thought about what their behavior might mean.

She tried to remember if *Mamm* had said anything about Leah being courted. Was it possible they had not told anyone yet? They looked so serious, it was difficult to believe they were planning to wait much longer to post their intentions.

But that doesn't make any sense. Zeke said he thought there might be something between them... until he met me. Just how long have they been keeping their relationship a secret?

"Zeke, how long ago did you think there might be something between you and Leah?" He frowned a little when she asked but then he seemed to be distracted with trying to remember.

"Well, she and I have grown up together. I have known her all my life. But it was only a few weeks ago that I drove her to one of our gatherings. Why?"

She shook her head a little before answering. "I was just trying to figure out how long she and Jacob have been seeing each other. They look mighty close, *jah?*"

His arm brushed hers as he turned to get a better look at the couple and Rebekah felt heat rush from the area on her arm and flood through her at even the quick, unexpected contact.

"*Jah,* they do look like they have been together for some time now. I do wish she had just told me. I would not have made such a big deal about showing up and asking her to *kumme* with me to the gathering," he said, before turning back to look at Rebekah.

"Not that I am sorry. Clearly, *Gotte* had other plans for me. Better plans. " He put a proprietary arm around her shoulders.

The young woman returned then with their drinks and they made their way back to the table. When they arrived, Rebekah realized that Zeke must have ordered for all of them. He was carrying three drinks, two of which he set on the table next to Jacob and Leah, who hardly looked up as he slid the heavy mugs across the small table to them.

He looked over at Rebekah and rolled his eyes just a

little, but he was smiling, so she figured it must be mostly for show. Then he held out one of the remaining two seats for her and she slid into it with a *"danki"* aimed in his direction.

After watching the two of them sit there and just stare into each others eyes for a few moments, Rebekah got up the nerve to ask the question she wanted to know the answer to, hoping it might shock the two of them into realizing there were other people around them.

"So, how long have the two of you been together?"

It was still several seconds before her question pierced the fog of affection that seemed to be surrounding them. They turned to look at her and she stifled a giggle as she realized they both had the appearance of young *kinner* who had been caught with a hand in the cookie jar. After several seconds, Jacob finally answered.

"We met when your *Mamm* arrived. She told you the story... right?" He stopped until she nodded her head. As he continued, she took a sip of her cocoa and was surprised at how *gut* it tasted. It was more like the recipe her *Grossmammi* used than anything she had expected in an *Englisch kaffe* shop. She sipped again as Jacob went on.

"When I went looking for help, their *haus* was the

closest one. I knocked at the door and Leah answered." He smiled over at Leah then and she spoke up.

"It was several *nachts* before he shined a light in my window."

"And I think it still took you several visits to realize that I was serious about you." Jacob added.

"*Jah,* that is true." Leah answered. "I had never been courted before." When she said that, Rebekah looked over at Zeke.

He did not look like he meant to argue with her, even though he had just said he had taken her to a gathering not so long ago. It must have been during the time when Leah did not know how serious Jacob was. Surely her new *schweschder* would not date two boys at once.

"Wait," Rebekah said as it began to dawn on her just how short a time that was. "That was just before Thanksgiving. You have only been together a little over a month."

Moving quickly must run in this family...

She looked over at Zeke as he slipped his hand into hers. There was something in his expression that made a tickling feeling explode in her stomach.

Expectation. Is he thinking that we will move that fast as well? She was still puzzling over it when Jacob spoke again.

"Your *mamm* and Leah's *dat* moved faster, *jah*?"

"*Jah,* and we have already decided that we will wait until fall to announce our intentions. There has been enough change in the families already for this year." Leah added.

"Not to mention... they have both been married and the bishop tends to make special considerations for those who have been widowed." Jacob turned to look at Leah, who smiled up at him, but Rebekah thought she could see tears in Leah's eyes.

Is she still mourning her Mamm?

Rebekah could not remember ever seeing Leah appear to be in mourning. She had been the picture of happiness and *gelassenheit* since Rebekah had arrived.

Leah shook her head a little and turned back to Rebekah and Zeke, her face suddenly serious.

"Zeke, I know I should have said something to you before now." But Zeke held up his hand to stop her.

"Leah, I have known you my entire life. I should have realized that you see me more as a *bruder*. You are not at fault. Besides," and his arm curled around Rebekah's shoulders again. "I believe I have found the one that *Gotte* intended for me."

Rebekah could not believe her ears. Was he saying what she thought he was saying? She looked over at him and the question was there in his eyes; there was no mistaking his feelings.

Rebekah felt herself nodding in his direction and she was surprised to realize there were tears in her own eyes. *It must be something about Windy Gap. Everyone moves fast here.* She felt laughter bubbling up inside of her, but she did everything she could to push it down. Now was certainly not the time for laughter.

Zeke squeezed her hand that he still held, and she did not think his smile could have gotten any bigger.

"So, next season for us as well, then?" he said to her so quietly, no one else could have heard, and she nodded again.

Then he surprised her by lifting the hand he held to his lips and brushing a quick kiss over her knuckles. Then he smiled at her over their joined hands and she felt a blush burning her cheeks again.

EIGHT

Rebekah woke before the first rays of light shone into the room, her heart so light, it felt as if she floated out of the bed. She moved over to the window, looking out onto the still-dark yard.

In the distance, she could just see a hint of light in the sky as it crept over the low hills. The wild array of pinks and purples reflected against a white blanket of snow that covered the land so that it was nearly impossible to tell where the ground ended and the sky began.

She smiled, thinking of how perfectly the colors reflected her mood. Her heart, which had been full of darkness and sadness, was filled with joy and light—a bright, beautiful light.

It was still difficult to believe it had all happened just the evening before. Less than a month ago, she had felt like she might never fit in here.

And then Leah suggested we go to town.

"Gut morning, Rebekah." Leah's voice behind her was filled with the same sort of delight that Rebekah felt.

She turned to her new *schweschder* with a smile. *"Gut* morning, Leah. It was a *gut nacht, jah?"*

Leah was already nodding. *"Jah,* a *wunderbaar gut nacht."* A moment later, she added, "you slept well?"

Rebekah nodded and turned to look out the window again, thinking back to when she had looked outside to see her cousin standing there with an arm slung over Zeke's shoulder like they were the best of *freinden.*

"Jah, very well. You?"

She looked back at her new *schweschder,* and Leah was nodding before Rebekah even finished the question, a wide, bright smile on her face. A moment later, Leah threw back the covers and swung her feet over the edge of the bed.

When she did not immediately rise, Rebekah realized this might be her only chance to ask the question that had plagued her since the day before—the only question that cast an apprehensive pall over the previous twenty-four hours.

"When do you think you will tell *Mamm* and your *Dat* about Jacob?" Rebekah hoped she was not over-stepping by asking the question, but she needed to know the answer. This was not an area where she could afford a mistake.

There were so many things about Windy Gap that were different from Hope Springs, and not having a lot of experience with dating to begin with, she worried she would do something silly, or even worse—embarrassing.

She would certainly not want to embarrass Zeke... or Leah... or Jacob.

"Oh, I don't know. I think I will let Jacob tell them when he feels the time is right."

Rebekah looked over at her new *schweschder* then. It was such a surprise to hear the same uncertainty in Leah's tone that she felt about Zeke.

"So, it is not the custom here to tell your parents about every boy you date... as soon as you begin to date?"

"Not at all." Leah was shaking her head as she answered, her expression suddenly serious. "Is that the way you did things in Ohio?"

Rebekah moved away from the window and settled herself on Leah's bed. "Can I be completely honest with you, Leah?"

Leah nodded and Rebekah went on.

"I never dated in Ohio, so I don't really know."

Leah was nodding again, and she picked up Rebekah's thought quickly enough. "And you didn't have older *bruders* and *schweschders* to watch and learn from..."

Now it was Rebekah's turn to nod. "And with *dat* sick all the time and *mamm* so busy taking care of him, there really was no one to ask for advice."

Leah took hold of both of Rebekah's hands then. "Do you mean to tell me that your date last *nacht* with Zeke was your first date?"

"Jah, it was."

Leah giggled before going on. "Well, you could not have picked a better boy that Zeke Hershberger for your first date. That is for certain. He is a very *gut* man."

Rebekah wanted to ask Leah if she had ever felt anything for him other than friendship, but had no idea how to word what she really wanted to know, and did not want to upset her new *schweschder*—not when they were getting along so well.

Fortunately, Leah answered her question with her next words. "I mean, it's not as if I have ever been interested in him that way, but I have known him for years. He is one of the best boys we have in the community... maybe *the best*."

Rebekah let out a breath she hadn't realized she was holding, smiling for the first time in several minutes. "And Jacob is certainly the best in my *aenti* and *onkel's* community."

Leah's face lit up at the mention of her cousin and Rebekah laughed a little. Leah looked as if she felt about Jacob, the way Rebekah felt about Zeke.

Suddenly she was very glad to have a *schweschder* to share all of this with, especially if it was not the norm to share news of her relationship with *mamm* so early.

.   .   .

Naomi looked up at the sound of footsteps on the stairs. She smiled when she saw that Rebekah and Leah had *kumme* down together, and that they were laughing together over something.

Both *maedels* were gesturing widely as they communicated in the silly short-hand of teenagers with a shared experience, in half sentences and giggles. It warmed her heart to see them getting on so well, especially given how difficult a time Rebekah had initially had, fitting in with such a large family.

Their trip into town must have been wunderbaar gut.

"*Gudemariye,* you two. It sounds to me like you both had a *wunderbaar* time in town yesterday."

Both *maedels* giggled again before answering. And then, when they did, their voices overlapped each other as they both starting with a breathless *jah,* which sent them into giggles again.

Naomi watched them laugh. It warmed her heart to see them, clutching onto each other, to hold each other upright. "I can see that the answer is *jah.* And it looks as if you are still having fun, *jah?*"

When they both started to answer at the same time again, and stopped, looking at each other with a smile, she went on. "Any special plans for today?"

This time, they did not speak at the same time. Rebekah looked to Leah, who spoke for them both. "We thought we would go into town again."

Rebekah did speak then, rushing to add, "after our chores are finished for the day."

Leah nodded her head in agreement, and then went on. "*Jah.* We met a few of the youth in town yesterday, but there might be more today since it is a bit warmer than usual for this time of year."

Naomi laughed. "Warmer... this is warmer weather than you usually have this time of year?"

Leah was already nodding, even as she was laughed. "Oh, *jah,* it is usually much colder this time of year." She laid a hand on Naomi's arm before going on. "I am sorry to say you have not seen the coldest weather we can have during this season."

"Truly?" Naomi could hardly believe what she was hearing. The weather she had encountered so far was much colder than anything in Ohio. It was difficult to believe it could be even colder here.

"*Jah.* When we get a blizzard, we could be snowbound for a week or more." Leah stepped back, smiling a little, as if trying to reassure Naomi.

She must have picked up on how worried I look.

"It really is not as bad as all that. I mean, our buggies will travel in weather that the *Englishers* will not go out in. It is just easier to stay put when the temperatures are at their coldest." She looked down then, her voice much quieter when she spoke again. "And it is never a *gut* idea to go out when there is almost no visibility."

Naomi wondered at the change in Leah's voice, but Rebekah spoke up then, effectively steering the conversation elsewhere. "What about worship? Do they still gather for *Gotte's* day?"

"Not usually. Not during a blizzard." A moment later, she added. "That is why nearly everyone goes into town when it is warm enough. When the blizzards *kumme,* you will be wishing you had taken every opportunity to go into town."

Rebekah took Naomi's hand. "Maybe you should *kumme* into town with us, *mamm.*"

Naomi thought about the long list of baking she had planned for the day. An outing with her *dochder*—and her new *dochder*—sounded like a *gut* idea. "You could be right, dear. Maybe it would be better to do our baking on the coldest days. It would certainly help to keep busy."

Rebekah spoke up again. *"Jah.* Having things to do will make the time go by quicker."

"Maybe I will go into town with you, then."

Leah giggled before adding, "Or mayhaps you and *dat* could go into town together, and Rebekah and I could take the small buggy. That way you can spend some time together."

Heat worked its way into Naomi's cheeks at Leah's words. She knew her new *dochder* did not mean what she was thinking, but she could not help the thoughts that rushed to mind at the thought of being alone with her new husband. *Ach, it makes me feel like a youth all over again.*

"That is a very *gut* idea, Leah. *Danki."* She turned back to breakfast with a wide smile.

Behind her, she could hear Leah and Rebekah move off toward the mud room, their footsteps sounding together in a happy, little pattern.

. . .

Leah smiled as she slipped on her outdoor boots. It was difficult to believe that only a couple of months ago, she had felt completely lost in the world. She had despaired of ever having a boy *kumme* calling. She had felt lost, and alone, and left behind, and like she would never understand what it was to be a woman.

And then Dat decided it was time to find a new frau.

Everything had changed the day a young man had *kumme* knocking on their door.

Heat rushed into her cheeks at the thought of Jacob and she was certain her smile widened. He was exactly the boy she had always wished for... prayed for... but been afraid to really expect. He was thoughtful and kind, understanding and intelligent, but also strong and dependable.

Even though she was secretly afraid to hope that it might mean he intended to make her his one day, it felt very much a possibility when he started telling her of his plans for the future. He had been working for years with their neighbor, an *Englisher* who bred and raised horses.

Jacob had told her just last week that the man had been planning to retire from the business for years, but he had no children to take it over and he was particular about how to handle his business. He did not want to just hand it over to a stranger who might not treat the horses right. That very same day, he had asked Jacob if he would be interested in taking over the business.

Jacob had excitedly shared the news with Leah, telling her that he had been praying for something like that to happen for some time. When he told her, it had felt different, not like something a young man would tell his girlfriend, more like something a man would share with the woman he intended to marry.

But Leah kept telling herself to wait, not to get too excited, not to expect too much. Not to push, but to wait on *Gotte's* timing—and on Jacob's.

So she was waiting... even though she wanted to be excited. She wanted to tell her new *schweschder* all about it. She wanted to tell her new *mamm,* her *dat,* and all of her *freinden.*

But still she waited. And she was determined to enjoy every bit of the time they were spending together now.

Her smile widened again, this time in relief, as she thought about their time in town today. *Nee,* Jacob would not be there. He would be working, but she knew that there was a *gut* chance that Zeke would be in town. He often had things to do in town in the afternoons, so at least Rebekah would have a chance to see him.

And Leah could finally stop feeling guilty every time she saw her childhood *freind.* Now they could just be *freinden,* with no worry about either expecting something different from the other.

He had Rebekah now. *And I have Jacob. And Dat has Naomi.* As the warmth spread again, different this time, spreading out from her heart, she looked up at her new *schweschder.*

Who could ever have thought things would have worked out this way? She knew the answer, of course.

Gotte. Gotte had known. He had always known.

NINE

Leah looked up in surprise when Rebekah spoke suddenly. They had turned onto the main road more than ten minutes ago and so far Rebekah had said nothing. Leah, uncertain of whether or not she should break the silence, had concentrated only on driving the buggy.

"So, what is the story with *Sew Sweet* and *Sew Nice?* There has to be a story behind those names, *jah?*"

Leah laughed before answering. It was almost exactly the same question that Naomi had asked after their first visit to town. "To understand that, you would have to know the Stutzman *schweschders* better."

"Like your *freind* Margaretta? She certainly does

have..." Rebekah stopped, clearly hunting around for a way to express her thoughts.

"It's *allrecht,* Rebekah." Leah laughed, thinking of her *freind's* odd sense of humor. "She certainly does have an odd way about her, even for an *Englischer,* but she is not one of the Stutzman *schweschders.* She just works for them."

"So, the Stutzman *schweschders* own *Sew Sweet* and *Sew Nice,* then?"

"*Jah.* They opened the shops a few years ago, after Abigail's husband died. Ruth has never married, though I have no idea why, since she is the best baker in the community."

Rebekah nodded, but said nothing, so Leah went on. "They both keep busy. *Sew Sweet* is almost always full of customers and Abigail teaches sewing and quilting classes three days a week at *Sew Nice.* Even some of our plain neighbors take her classes to learn her techniques."

"Is the quilt on the wall of *Sew Sweet* one of hers, then?"

Leah was already nodding. "*Jah.* She has certainly been blessed with a *wunderbaar* talent."

"Maybe she could help me, then. I am the absolute worst quilter."

"I am sure that is not true." She had helped to

unpack some of the quilts they had brought with then from Ohio and she found it difficult to believe that Rebekah could not be at least as talented as her *mamm* and *grossmammi* were at quilting.

"Oh, *jah. Mamm* and *Grossmammi* have tried to teach me, but I am hopeless." She shrugged, but Leah could see that there was no arguing with her, so she changed tactics.

"Have you ever wondered if you are maybe judging yourself too harshly?"

Rebekah opened her mouth to speak, but stopped before saying anything. She closed her mouth with a little "hmm" and then, a moment later, started again. "What do you mean?"

Leah smiled before answering. "I mean, you are looking at the quilts your *mamm* and *grossmammi* have made, and you are expecting your work to be as *gut* as theirs, *jah?*"

Again, Rebekah started to speak, only to stop herself. She shook her head and Leah turned her attention back to the horses, giving her new *schweschder* time to think.

They were nearly to town before she spoke again. "Why should I not expect my work to be just like *Mamm's* and *Grossmammi's?* Is that not how teaching works? I am supposed to learn to do what they are doing, *jah?*"

Leah nodded again. "I used to think so, *jah*. My older *schweschders* tried many times to teach me to quilt... and cook... and to do many other things... the way they do them. But I am not them, so I cannot always do things as they do."

Rebekah spoke up then. "I am glad you found your own way. You are a *wunderbaar* cook."

Leah secretly felt delighted with her *schweschder's* remark, but shook it off, lest she be prideful. *"Danki.* I would not be though, if I had tried to be my *schweschders*. They have different ways of doing almost everything. I had to take what they taught me about the basics and then find my own way. That is what you must do."

Leah gave Rebekah a moment to think that over before adding, "You must also realize that they have been quilting for many years. There is *nee* substitute for experience."

"I am certain you are right about that." She let out a deep sigh and then went on. "I suppose I should try again."

"Jah. You should."

They rode in silence for several minutes. And then, just as they arrived in town, Leah added, "You could always take one of Abigail's classes. It could not hurt, *jah?"*

"Do you think *Mamm* would mind, though?"

Leah looked over at Rebekah in surprise. *Did she really just ask my opinion about her mamm?*

She started to answer, but stopped herself. Truly, she had not known her new *mamm* long enough to know the correct answer.

And if Rebekah is worried about how Naomi will react... Her thoughts trailed off when Rebekah spoke up again.

"I suppose it wouldn't hurt to just mention it some time."

Leah nodded as she slowed the team a bit so that she could turn into the special parking lot that was laid out with buggies in mind. When she had parked and set the brake, she looked around for familiar buggies, but saw none. She started to say something to Rebekah, but she was already climbing down from the buggy, so Leah did the same.

At least we can go into Sew Sweet and warm up... and have a treat.

Then perhaps they could go to *Sew Nice* and find out what Abigail's upcoming class schedules were. There was no point in wasting a trip into town.

.   .   .

Rebekah looked around at the other buggies in the parking lot, not entirely certain she would even recognize Jacob's or Zeke's if it was parked beside them. It might be silly to expect that she would see Zeke in town, after spending hours with him last night, but she could not help the excitement bubbling up within her just at the possibility.

She stepped down onto the hard-packed snow that covered the ground, still looking around her, hoping to catch a glimpse of a familiar face. When Leah walked around the buggy, and she still had not caught sight of Zeke or his buggy, Rebekah sighed a little, but quickly put a smile on her face, locking arms with her new *schweschder*. A moment later, they set off together in the direction of the nearest store.

"I hope you don't mind. I need to pick up a few things at the hardware store for Benjamin... well, really it's for Caleb, but Benjamin will be doing the work for him, so..." She shrugged a little and Rebekah had to smile, thinking of poor Caleb.

How awful it must be for him. Granted, she was new to the very active Fisher household, but she already knew how hard everyone worked day and *nacht*. And to be forced to sit still, not even allowed to put enough weight on his leg so he could go to the bathroom by himself, must be torture.

However, the thought also gave Rebekah the opening she had been waiting for—hoping for.

"What sort of stories does Caleb enjoy? Perhaps we should stop in at the library and pick him up some books to read. Maybe it would help distract him."

Leah laughed, and for a moment, Rebekah was worried she had said something wrong. Did their community frown on reading fiction? Did Caleb think reading was something silly? *Does Leah?* Had she misjudged her new *schweschder?* And, if she had, what would Leah do with the information now?

"The only books Caleb reads are about horse breeding." Leah laughed again before going on. "When we were younger, he spent a lot of time reading books about kids and their horses and all the adventures they went on, but..." She shrugged and then added, "Now, though... well, he doesn't read anything that is fiction."

Then she turned to Rebekah with a sneaky sort of smile. "Maybe we should get him some books at the library. If he stopped reading them because he didn't have time, well, he certainly does now."

Rebekah breathed a sigh of relief. She had not made a mistake after all.

And now I will get to see the library.

"We will have to do the library last. I dare not take

books into *Sew Sweet* again." Something about Leah's tone sounded as if she spoke from experience. Rebekah wanted to ask why, but her *schweschder* spoke again before she got the chance.

"One time... just one time, I leave a tiny bit of icing on one of the books." She was talking to herself more than Rebekah at that point, but it was not hard to see where the story was going.

Rebekah followed as Leah walked into the large hardware store, still talking to herself, though now it was much more difficult to make out. Though Rebekah did hear something about *bruder* and *trouble maker* in her comments.

She smiled to herself. This was a side of Leah she had not yet seen. Before Caleb's injury, she had seen some teasing between him and Leah, but none since. There must be a history of teasing between the two, but Caleb had clearly been in no mood for teasing since.

Not that I can blame him.

It was not at all a surprise that the once active young man would be a bit stir crazy, confined to the *haus* and to the small guest bedroom downstairs, unable to care for his horses or do any of the daily chores that were likely as secondary to him as breathing.

Rebekah followed Leah as she made her way

through the large store, filling a sturdy basket with the items she pulled from shelves and hooks. Knowing only enough about horses to feed them, hook them up to the small buggy back home, and ride a little, Rebekah had *nee* idea what Caleb could possibly need with all of these things, but she didn't ask either, in case Leah was no more the wiser.

Moving to another part of the store, Leah took out a second list. "And now I will get the things *Dat* asked me to pick up for him." These things Leah picked up, Rebekah paid a lot more attention to, knowing they were likely things Samuel needed for his wood carving.

Zeke might not use all of the same tools in his work, but making furniture surely was not all that different from wood carving, so she was excited to see what sorts of things Zeke might use in his work.

She looked at the different sizes of chisels and hammers, and she wondered how many of these types of tools Zeke might use when working with his furniture. Were all these different things only needed when doing delicate carving or would a furniture maker use them, too?

She wanted to ask Zeke when she saw him again, but she was still hesitant about their relationship. If she counted their meeting in town yesterday, they had only been out together twice. Was that too soon to begin thinking of the possibility that things might be leading somewhere serious?

She turned to follow Leah and nearly collided with the person coming up behind her. Strong hands... familiar hands... took hold of her and kept her from losing her balance.

Heat rushed into her cheeks with the realization of where her thoughts had just been.

"Careful, Rebekah. This is not a *gut* place to trip." His deep voice held enough concern, mixed with something else that made her want to blush again—for an entirely different reason—to make her earlier worries feel silly.

"You're right. I should have been looking where I was going." She felt steady on her feet now, but noticed that he did not let go of her. Instead, he kept a light grip on her hand.

"You came in with Leah, *jah?*" He asked the question, but since he must have seen Leah walk by him, Rebekah only nodded.

"I came in to replace a chisel. Tom has sharpened the one I've been using many times, but I think it has finally had enough." He stepped to the side for a moment, still not letting go of her hand, and Rebekah followed his movements with her eyes as he plucked a chisel from the wall behind her.

"What else do you need to do while you are in town?"

Rebekah hesitated for a moment. Leah had wanted to go to *Sew Sweet,* but what if she had other plans for their trip that she had not mentioned.

Fortunately, Leah came around the corner behind Zeke just then. "Hi, Zeke. Imagine bumping into you here." Leah's smile told Rebekah that she was not one bit surprised to find Zeke here... in the hardware store... in the section they had visited to buy tools for Samuel... buying a chisel for his work.

"Hi Leah." His tone made it plain that he was not the least surprised either. "What else do you and Rebekah have to do in town today?"

Leah only grinned. "We were about to head over to *Sew Sweet* for a treat and some cocoa. Do you have time to join us?"

Zeke looked back at Rebekah, the question obvious in his expression.

"That would be *wunderbaar*... if you have time."

Zeke smiled. "I have time." Then he turned back to Leah. "How much more shopping do you need to do here?"

"I'm all done, so we are ready to go whenever you are. How much more shopping do you have to do?"

He held up the chisel in answer. "None at all. This

was the only thing I came in for." With that, he turned and headed toward the front of the store, still not letting go of Rebekah's hand.

She happily followed along. Leah grinned as they passed. Then Rebekah could hear her walking along behind them as they moved to the front of the store. Zeke made quick work of paying for his chisel and Rebekah could not help but wonder if the look the store's owner gave her meant that he knew precisely why Zeke was holding so tightly to her hand.

There was little time to worry over it though, because the moment the man handed over Zeke's receipt, he stepped away from the counter, and headed for the door.

TEN

Zeke let go of Rebekah's hand long enough to hold the door for her and then for Leah, calling out an reply to the shop owner's goodbye before stepping through the door and letting it swing shut behind him. And then they were on the sidewalk. Looking down the street, Rebekah could see a sign about a block away for *Sew Sweet.*

"Nowhere else you need to go now?" Zeke asked again. Leah shook her head. *"Nee.* All I needed was those few things from the hardware store." She started to move toward *Sew Sweet, then* stopped.

"Oh, I forgot. Rebekah wanted to stop in at the library to pick out some books for Caleb, but that can wait until last."

Zeke nodded, then set off in the direction of the cafe before asking, "How is Caleb doing? If he is bored, he must be feeling well. And for certain he is going mad with the forced inactivity."

"Well..." Rebekah started to answer charitably, but Leah spoiled it by laughing. "He is, *jah.* He keeps trying to convince *Dat* that he should at least be able to limp his way out to the barn to visit the new foal."

"Surely your *Dat* is not going to let him..." He left the question hanging, but Leah was already answering. *"Nee.* He is not so easily fooled. The doctor said three weeks until he can return and have it checked, and no weight on the entire leg before then, and that is what we are going to do, whether Caleb likes it or not."

"Gut. I did not think your *Dat* would take a chance like that."

"And with so many people around day and *nacht,* it isn't as if he could sneak and do it anyway." Rebekah realized when she'd finished, that it was possible her comment might sound a tad harsh, and she started to apologize, but if Leah or Zeke was offended, neither one showed it.

"Your *haus* has always been a busy one."

Leah nodded before adding, *"Jah.* Even the older ones who are married are there nearly every day." She turned to Rebekah then, putting an arm around her new *schweschder's* shoulder. "I do not know how Rebekah stands all the craziness of our *haus.*"

With both Leah and Zeke watching her so intently, Rebekah was very cautious of her answer. "It is certainly different. That much is true."

Leah laughed and squeezed her shoulders tightly before letting go, and Zeke squeezed her hand gently again, giving her a smile that told her he understood her.

She was glad to see the understanding in his eyes. She had worried over the answer for his benefit as much as Leah's, since he came from nearly as large a family. Though, of his six *bruders,* Zeke was the youngest, so his *haus* was likely much quieter than the Fishers', especially since two of them lived in Ohio with their families and would not be constantly dropping in.

Still, I would not want him to think that I would be opposed to large families.

Truth be told, there had been too many times when she was growing up for her to have kept count, that she had wished for *bruders* and *schweschders.*

If only Dat had not been so sick... she pushed the thought away. She had a large family now and she would just have to learn to handle the constant busyness.

Just then, Zeke let go of her hand to open the door to *Sew Sweet.* Leah followed her in, but rushed over to hug her *Englischer freind,* who came out from behind the counter to return Leah's hug.

"I suppose we should find a table for three." Zeke spoke softly, his voice surprisingly near her ear.

She smiled and nodded, even as her body warmed and the nerves all along her neck went crazy from his closeness. He took her hand again and led her over to a large table than she and Leah had occupied before, one with four chairs.

Rebekah wanted to hope that one of Leah's *freinden* would ask her to sit with them—then it would almost be like another date for her and Zeke—but she could not be so uncharitable to her new *schweschder.*

"Cocoa?" Zeke asked, holding out Rebekah's chair for her. And, when she nodded, he added, "Anything else?"

"I don't really know. I didn't get to choose last time. Leah's *freind* brought us something special."

"*Jah,* and chances are, she will again." He stepped away, before turning back to her. "Save my seat." And he moved toward the counter with a wink in her direction.

Rebekah felt her smile widen and the warmth that his earlier words had stirred within her spread, filling her heart and making her feel *wunderbaar.*

It was several minutes before Leah and Zeke returned, each laden down with drinks and plates.

Leah must have noticed Rebekah's hand resting lightly on the chair Zeke had just vacated, because she set one plate and one mug down in front of the chair across from her's before sliding a plate in front of Rebekah.

Before Zeke could set down the two heavy mugs and plate he was carrying, Leah had pulled out her own chair and sat down, picking up her mug and blowing across the top of the steamy liquid within.

"Hope you like Lava Fudge Cake." Leah said, taking a cautious sip of her cocoa.

Rebekah looked down at the dessert sitting in front of her. It was a small, chocolate cake in the shape of a mountain, with chocolate drizzled over top of it.

"What's the Lava Fudge part?" She asked, poking it gently with her fork.

"It's inside." Leah answered. "It's something new that Margaretta has been working on. The cake is filled with warm, liquid fudge." She poked hers then, and a thick chocolate flowed out of the hole she had created. "Mmmm. Perfect for a cold, winter day."

Rebekah poked hers and watched the thick liquid flow out onto the plate. She had to admit, it did look delicious. She poked the cake again, pulling a small portion away and dipping it into the liquid fudge before lifting the fork to her mouth.

Just as she put the bite into her mouth, Leah's *freind* appeared beside the table. "Well, what do you think? Isn't it to die for?"

Rebekah didn't really care for the choice of words Leah's *freind* used, but she nodded anyway, thinking it must be an *Englischer* way of saying something was sinfully *gut*. The spongy cake and warm fudge in her mouth tasted absolutely delicious.

Leah took a bite then, and so did Zeke. And, if the expressions on their faces were anything to go by, they were thinking the same thing she was about how *wunderbaar* the dessert tasted.

Leah was the first to speak. "I was going to say that this may be a bit too fancy for the cafe to sell, but whether it is or not, you should have no trouble selling it."

"Well, actually, this is something that Miranda is thinking of selling at Higher Grounds, so I guess that could be a really good thing."

While Leah and Margaretta chatted, Rebekah took another bite, enjoying the combination of chocolate and fudge. At the moment, she couldn't think of anything nicer than sitting here next to Zeke, close enough to almost be touching, while enjoying this special treat.

. . .

Rebekah sat beside Leah on Leah's bed, both of them fully dressed with their hair still pinned up, even though the house around them was dark... watching the window for a telltale beam of light.

She took turns looking from the window to the clock on the small table and back to the window, wondering why she felt so much more impatient tonight.

Leah's voice nearly made her jump, even though her words came out in a whisper of sound. "Are you feeling as antsy as I am?"

"*Jah.* I wonder what it is."

Leah shook her head before answering, "I cannot think of why we should be. I do not think I was this anxious the first time I waited to see Jacob's light."

"Right. And it isn't like this is only your second date." She laughed a little at herself. This was not exactly her second date with Zeke, but it was in fact the second evening she had sat here, waiting to see a light shine in the window. If she were the only one feeling as if the clock were ticking backwards, it would make sense.

But why is Leah feeling the same way?

Fortunately, they had no more time to worry over it because at that moment two beams of light flashed through the glass and danced across the wall behind them.

They were both off the bed in a flash and rushing over to the window. Like the first time, Jacob and Zeke stood side by side, identical grins on their handsome faces. Rebekah waved as Leah motioned to the porch, holding up just five fingers this time.

Then they were making their way out into the hall, moving quietly down the stairs. Rebekah had a moment to be grateful that Leah was in front because she waved her hands in the air near the bottom of the stairs, reminding Rebekah about the step that they needed to skip over.

Ach. I had forgotten all about that.

Following Leah's lead, she stepped carefully over the creaky stair and then rushed toward the back door.

They were both fighting giggles as they struggled into their boots and coats—and again Rebekah was thankful that Leah finished first because she opened the back door oh-so-carefully—and quietly. Quickly they slipped through the opening.

The guys were already standing at the edge of the porch, reaching up to lift them down. They had barely touched the ground before they were rushing down the driveway, flashlight beams bouncing madly over the gravel driveway as Rebekah and Leah finally let loose the giggles they had struggled with ever since they had closed their bedroom door and begun listening for sounds of the household settling in for sleep.

Halfway down the gravel drive, Jacob voiced the question that she had been asking herself all evening.

"Not that I am complaining, but what has gotten into you two tonight?"

Rebekah started to speak, to tell her cousin that they had no idea, just as Leah lost her footing. Fortunately, Jacob was on one side of her and Zeke was on the other, with Rebekah on his other side. They both took hold of an arm, keeping her from falling. Then Jacob put both arms around her, steadying her on her feet.

Zeke turned to Rebekah, presumably to be certain she was steady. A moment after Jacob commented, "maybe we should walk more slowly now," Zeke said, "I must admit, I have been thinking the same thing."

They all slowed, though neither young man offered any suggestions as to the unexplained restlessness that was affecting both of the girls.

They were nearly to the buggies when Zeke spoke up. "Hey! Could it be all that chocolate?"

"Chocolate?" Rebekah looked up at him in confusion. How could chocolate have anything to do with restlessness?

"*Jah.* I didn't think of it right away, but then I remembered that when I got home this afternoon, I was mighty energetic—more than normal. I thought it was..." He coughed a little, and Rebekah felt heat rush to her cheeks at the look he aimed in her direction before rushing on. "Anyway, maybe it was the chocolate."

"*Ach.* You are right." Leah laughed before adding, "I did not even put it together until now, but I should have. Especially since this has happened before."

Rebekah felt as if she was missing something, but before she could ask what Leah meant, she answered the question.

"Margaretta is always having me taste new things she is wanting to sell at the bakery." There was a hint of red in Leah's cheeks that clearly had nothing to do with the cold weather. "I do not know why I never put the two events together. I have been her test audience for over a year now."

Jacob squeezed Leah in a swift hug. "Don't feel bad, sweetheart. It took all four of us really, to figure out what had happened."

Rebekah turned away then, looking anywhere but at

the couple. The look Leah and Jacob shared felt entirely too private for others to be watching.

Zeke squeezed her hand. When she turned to look up at him, heat rushed back into her cheeks at the expression on his face.

Without realizing it, Rebekah leaned forward, not thinking about anything beyond getting closer to Zeke. Thankfully she stopped when Leah's voice broke the silence. "So then, should we skip Higher Grounds tonight?"

Rebekah had no idea how to interpret the serious expression on Zeke's face, but Leah's *naerfich* laughter told her that she was aware of what she had just interrupted. While Rebekah was certain her new *schweschder* had not intended to do so, she was a bit relieved to be sure... especially after what Zeke had told her the previous evening about his intentions on kissing.

Fortunately, Jacob spoke up then, breaking the tension smoothly. "I think we could still go to Higher Grounds. This is not a *nacht* I would want to sit outside anywhere."

A shiver accompanied his words and Rebekah found herself nodding. Her cousin was exactly right. *It would likely not be a very gut idea to be sitting all alone with Zeke... anywhere.*

"*Jah.* Being inside where it is nice and warm sounds mighty *gut* to me." *It won't hurt either that we will be surrounded by people.*

The idea of being alone with Zeke excited Rebekah—and worried her, too. Everything was moving along so quickly she wasn't sure at times what to think of it all.

Zeke looked down at Rebekah before replying. The expression on his face was impossible to decipher. She couldn't decide if she was relieved or not when he said, "Higher Grounds it is, then."

She smiled and nodded, but said nothing else as he turned and headed toward the buggies, her hand still tucked tightly in his.

ELEVEN

Naomi watched as members of her new family filed by, each carrying a large basket filled with food to contribute to lunch. It felt *gut* to be part of such a large family, to feel needed again, to have the love of so many family members—and to see her *dochder* beginning to fit in as well.

Rebekah walked by with Leah and Lillian, and it warmed Naomi's heart to see all three of them smiling and chattering away as if they had always been *schweschders.*

While the girls climbed up into the larger family buggy, Peter and Matthew pulled the wagon around, a pile of blankets already in the back.

Benjamin and Elam came through the front door a moment later, carrying Caleb between them. Naomi wanted to chide her new son for the look of annoyance on his face, but then she reminded herself of how long it had taken John to admit that he needed help.

He had taken so long to even share the news of his sickness with her. And then he had hurt himself several times before he had finally admitted that he would need help doing things—things he had never had any trouble with before.

The male ego—even a plain man's—was a fragile thing, although they would never admit such a thing.

She resisted the urge to comment on Caleb's sour expression. She also refrained from fussing over him once Benjamin and Elam had settled him in the wagon. He had enough sense to know he would need to cover up.

Just as the wagon pulled away, Samuel appeared at the top of the porch steps, holding out a hand to her— and with a smile, she moved over to him, taking his hand and descending with him to the waiting buggy.

The entire drive, Naomi thought about all the amazing blessings that *Gotte* had showered upon them over the last few months; finding Samuel and his *wunderbaar* family, being joined together with—and accepted by—that same family. Not only had his *kinner* made her feel welcome, they treated her as if she had always been one of them.

She had worried over Rebekah during the move to Samuel's home in Windy Gap, but everyone had made her *dochder* just as welcome. Why, she and Leah were closer than Rebekah had been with anyone in Hope Springs.

Then there were the blessings she had seen after joining the Fisher family. For sure and for certain, they were an active bunch who got into all sorts of minor scrapes and accidents, but it was obvious that *Gotte* had been taking special care of Caleb. Not only was it a miracle in her mind that he had survived such an ordeal, but he had not lost his leg. That was a miracle no one argued with.

Then there was the miracle going on in Leah's life. Not only had she connected with Rebekah, which Naomi had worried plenty over; she had also lost all of the sadness that had been a constant cloud over her when Naomi had first met the young *maedel*. In no time at all, she had become a sweet, content, cheerful and bubbly young woman who was a joy to be around.

There was no doubt in Naomi's mind that all of it was a blessing from *Gotte*. There was simply no other explanation for it all.

When they pulled up to the Hershberger *haus,*

Samuel leaned in to gave Naomi a quick kiss before she could climb out with their *dochders* to take their baskets in. "I'll park at the barn and see if the boys need any help getting Caleb settled."

The butterflies that skittered through her at his closeness was another blessing she delighted in. Even though she had decided against marrying John's *bruder,* it had been about more than just wanting to make the choice herself. *Jah,* she had hoped she might find *lieb* again, but she could never have anticipated feeling like a giggly school-girl again—not at her age. Not when she had a *dochder* who was nearly grown. Not when she had already been married nearly two decades.

It was a delightful benefit, and not one she was likely to take for granted. She smiled up at Samuel, leaning in so that she could return the kiss. "I will miss you."

At the sound of giggles behind them, and Samuel's answering grin, she was not at all surprised to hear delighted laughter—almost a giggle—coming from deep within her as well.

He kissed her again before she turned to climb down and she snuggled into *lieb* like a warm blanket as she stepped down and carefully stepped on the frozen ground.

Slowly she made her way into the Hershberger's *haus,* following Leah, Rebekah, and several other ladies from the community. Before she walked through the kitchen doorway, she stopped to listen to the sounds of the ladies as they chatted, walking back and forth carrying food and plates and other supplies for the large meal.

. . .

The third time Leah nudged Rebekah, she realized she must be a little too obvious about staring out the window, watching Zeke as he carried benches into the barn. As she watched, he stopped to help the elder members of the community from their buggies and chatted with some of the young boys who looked as if they would never be able to sit still through the entire worship.

When one of the younger *maedels* giggled behind her and turned away a little too quickly, just as Rebekah looked in her direction, she realized she had given everyone in the room something to talk about.

Oh well, at least they do not know which young man I am interested in. It could be any of them out there.

At that point, she forced herself to turn away from the window. She might have given them a clue that she was interested, but that was all they knew, and according to Leah, that was all well and *gut.*

"You do realize, your *mamm* is likely to figure out that you are being courted if you keep that up. Your face gives you away." Leah whispered the words near Rebekah's ear, and Rebekah felt heat fill her cheeks in response.

"Also, if you keep staring so intently, someone will figure out who it is you are looking at." Patting her *schweschder's* arm, Leah then turned and walked away.

You are just lucky, Leah Fisher, that the boy you like is not here.

Rebekah had no doubts that her new *schweschder* would be doing exactly what she was doing if it were Jacob out there within sight.

Fortunately, no one confronted her about which young man she was interested in, and as far as she could tell, *Mamm* either did not pick up on it, or she had decided not to bring it up while they were surrounded by the entire community.

Whatever the reason, Rebekah worked twice as hard, trying to do anything she could to distract herself from looking out the window again... to the point that Leah had to pull her away from the table where she was trying to find room for one more platter of food when it was time for them to find their seats.

All through the singing, the preaching, the prayers, the *mamms* taking their little ones out when they made a fuss or needed a change, and the announcements, and more singing, Rebekah forced herself not to look over to where the young men were sitting.

She knew for a certain that if she looked, she would not be able to look away from Zeke's face. For certain, it would be long enough that anyone watching would be able to figure out who it was she was interested in. And then the information would get back to *Mamm... and she will know...* And then it will stop being about fun and just getting to know each other and would become serious and someone would be wanting to know what Zeke's intentions are.

And the whole thing could get ruined...

So she didn't look. She sat quietly, trying to listen intently, but certain that she would never be able to remember anything that was said later if anyone were to ask.

When the worship was over, she stood with everyone else and turned to follow Leah, to help prepare the meal. As her eyes met Zeke's from across the room, his smile warmed her from the inside out, and she stopped caring if everyone knew that she was for sure and for certain already halfway in love with him.

She wanted nothing more than to stand right where she was and go on looking at him forever. And she would have... if Leah had not pulled her away.

"Rebekah, we have to go and help. *Kumme*. There is plenty of time for that later." And with a laugh, she tugged on Rebekah's arm until she was forced to move.

Reluctantly, she looked away from Zeke's warm smile and allowed Leah to pull her away.

"The two of you certainly are *verhuddelt* each other, that is for sure." Leah laughed again and then added, "You have seen him two *nachts* and two days in a row. Is that not enough for you?"

Rebekah thought about it for a moment, and then said precisely what she was thinking. *"Nee.* It is not." Then she was struck by inspiration. "Would it be enough for you, if Jacob were here?"

Leah started to answer, but the words never came. Instead she closed her mouth and looked off in the distance, more likely as not in the direction of Jacob's district, obviously thinking it over long and hard before answering. *"Nee.* It probably would not be."

Rebekah nodded, pulling Leah's arm, since now she had stopped moving forward. Leah laughed. *"Allrecht. Allrecht.* You have a *gut* point."

"I know I do." After a moment, she relented, admitting to herself that Leah had a point, too. "But you are right, too. I do not need to make it so obvious. I certainly would not want to give anyone here a reason a talk about me."

Leah started to speak again, probably to ask what Rebekah meant, but again, she closed her mouth without saying a word. Instead, she linked arms with Rebekah and together they walked toward the *haus*.

After a moment, Rebekah spoke up. "Besides, for now, it is enough for me to know that I am helping prepare the meal in his kitchen, where he sits and eats and spends time with his family."

Leah laughed in answer as they made their way into the Hershberger *haus*.

TWELVE

Rebekah made her way into the Hershberger barn, looking around for Leah as she did so. *Where has she got to now?*

It was one thing to ignore Zeke all through the worship service, and then through the afternoon meal, but here... at the youth gathering... at his *haus*... everyone would know something was up between them —just as if they spent the entire evening together.

Ach. I wish I was better at all this gegisch dating nonsense.

"Hot cocoa?" Zeke's familiar voice had the hairs on her neck standing straight up and her insides doing a crazy sort of dance.

"Jah, danki. Hot cocoa would be *wunderbaar."* She took the cup he offered her, even though she knew she would not need the hot liquid to warm her insides. All she needed was to see the intensity of his expression when he looked at her.

Ach. Where is Leah when I need her. I do not know what I am supposed to do now.

An internal battle raged within her. Should she take the chance on showing everyone here just how much she cared for him, or should she try to be distant and cool, not allowing anyone to guess that they had been seeing each other?

"I can practically see the wheels turning in that head of yours. You are wondering if it is acceptable for you to spend time with me, *jah?"*

Rebekah gasped at how accurate his words were. Somehow he had known precisely what she had been thinking. *How does he do that?*

"How do you—? You must tell me how you do that."

But he was already shaking his head. "Where would be the fun in that?"

She could not help herself. She laughed. "Well, I would not want to be responsible for taking away your fun." And when he laughed, she forgot for a moment that she was worrying over whether or not she was meant to show her feelings for him.

"By the way, if you are looking for Leah, I believe she went for a walk with Jacob."

"Jacob?"

Zeke was already nodding. *"Jah.* He showed up about ten minutes ago. She was rushing out to meet him as I was walking to the barn with your cocoa."

"She must have told him about the youth gathering last *nacht."*

Zeke nodded again. "Funny that she did not think to mention it to you."

"Well, she wasn't sure if I would *kumme* to the gathering. In the past, I was never interested in them. I didn't want to *kumme* tonight. She practically insisted." Rebekah noticed that Zeke was not looking right at her. "I don't suppose you had anything to do with that."

"Who? Me?" He looked at her then—and she could see by the expression on his handsome face that he had known all about it—maybe it had even been his idea.

"Why did you not tell me about it yourself? I would have *kumme* if you had asked me."

At least he had the *gut* sense to look a bit sorry. "You are right. I should not have sprung the gathering on you." When he reached for her hand, she allowed him to take it, but she did not soften her own expression.

"I really wanted you to *kumme* and I was afraid you

would not. It is not as if we lied to you or anything. We just..."

"Did not trust me to make my own decision." Rebekah finished for him.

"Again, you are right. I am very sorry." When she said nothing, he went on. "I can drive you home right now if you would prefer."

She almost wanted to say yes, just to set him straight, but she did not wish to leave... or to go home, so she decided to let him have a bit of his own medicine, before letting him off the hook. She relaxed her shoulders and smiled. "You can drive me home—" she held up a hand when he started to interrupt, "when the gathering is over."

He smiled then and tucked her hand around his arm, heading for the large table that was loaded down with desserts.

"*Gut*. Then we must have something to eat. My *bruders* will have the sled out soon for rides and you do not want to miss the chocolate chip cookies *Mamm* made. They will be gone all too soon." As he talked, he led her over to the table. He handed her a plate, then began filling his own as he moved alongside the selection of snacks and treats.

When Rebekah spotted several desserts she had seen at *Sew Sweet,* she looked around for Leah's

Englischer freind. Zeke must have seen her looking around and guessed who she was searching for. "*Jah,* Margaretta is around here somewhere."

"Does someone invite her just for her treats or—" She stopped, realizing as soon as she asked the question that it might sound rude. but she hoped Zeke would understand her curiosity about it.

Zeke laughed before answering. "I think, *jah,* that someone might have invited her the first time for the *wunderbaar* treats they hoped she would bring, but we have made it plain since then that she is welcome anytime, whether she brings desserts or not."

He laughed again before adding, "you have seen how busy *Sew Sweet* is. It is always that busy. Nearly everyone in the community stops in when they are in town. And many of our youth are *gut freinden* with Margaretta. They expect her to *kumme* to as many gatherings as she can."

Rebekah nodded, relieved to hear how close the community ties were to the young woman. Back in Hope Springs, no *Englischer* would ever have attended one of their youth gatherings.

Not because they weren't invited though...

She could remember all the times she had tried to talk her *freind* from the library into attending one of their gatherings. She had never *kumme,* though there were times Rebekah had been sure she wanted to.

Careful to avoid anything with a lot of chocolate, Rebekah selected several treats and snacks. Zeke put several chocolate chip cookies on her plate before she could pick them up herself. Before they moved away from the table, he put several other treats on her plate as well.

"Zeke, stop that. Do you want me to be as *gegisch* as I was the other *nacht?*"

He only laughed.

She shook her head at his silliness, but followed him when he made his way to a bench near the large, barn doors. The first thing she bit into, once she'd settled herself on the bench next to him, was one of his *mamm's* cookies.

· · ·

He could not help himself. When Rebekah bit into one of *Mamm's* cookies and let out a little "mmm", he was suddenly very aware of how close to him she sat on the bench. Their hips were nearly touching and he was certain he could feel heat reaching out to him all along her arm, which was no more than an inch away from his.

Never before had his resolve... to wait... to kiss the

young woman he was about to marry, felt so difficult to follow through on. None of the other *maedels* in the community had ever held his interest the way Rebekah did. Truly, he had never expected to find a young woman quite so appealing to him, who appeared to feel the same for him.

That she seemed to have no idea how captivating she was only added to his attraction to her. It was nearly impossible for him to believe he had only known her a matter of days. She was everything he had always wanted in a *frau*.

He had nearly given up hope of finding a young woman in this district—or any of the ones nearby—who did not know him only as the skinny klutz who had bloomed much later than all of his other *freinden*. And just as he had given up, here she was.

Gotte truly does work in mysterious ways.

"Zeke, these cookies are amazing!" Her sweet voice interrupted his thoughts and he turned to her with a smile.

Everyone agreed that his *Mamm's* cookies were the best in three districts, but it was always a delight to hear.

"*Danki,* Rebekah. I will tell her you said so."

Before he could say anything else, Rebekah's cousin came through the doors, with Leah tucked under one arm. He must have spotted Zeke immediately because he changed direction and raised a hand in greeting. Zeke stood to greet his new *freind.*

"Zeke, *wie geht's?*"

"*Gut,* Jacob. And you?"

"Very *gut.* And glad to be here." Jacob looked over at Leah beside him with an expression that mirrored much of how Zeke felt whenever he thought about Rebekah.

Leah leaned in a bit closer to Jacob before answering. *"Jah,* everything is *gut."* Leah looked down at Rebekah—who was looking down at her plate while she chewed on a peanut butter cookie—and then back at Zeke. "Has she forgiven me yet?"

He almost wanted to tell her no, and take her to task for convincing him it would be a *gut* idea, but Rebekah spoke up then.

"I am not certain if I am ready to forgive you, Leah Fisher. It was not a nice thing that you did."

Leah looked surprised. "You know I only did it for you—and for Zeke. I didn't want to take a chance that you would refuse to *kumme."*

When Rebekah didn't speak again, Leah laughed softly. "That is fine, Rebekah. You forgive me when you are ready." And she pulled Jacob away toward the food tables.

Zeke turned back to Rebekah, ready to apologize again for his part in this, but she was smiling. He sat back down on the bench next to her, bewildered by her odd behavior.

"Rebekah, is everything *allrecht?*"

She quickly nodded. *"Jah,* Zeke. Everything is *gut*. I am fine. As much as I want to be upset with Leah for not telling me about this evening, I know she really was just trying to help. How can I be angry with her for that?"

"Could that mean you are no longer angry with me as well?" He almost didn't want to ask the question—what if she said no?

But he knew he had to ask. He had to know.

"I was never really angry with you, Zeke. I was mostly surprised, and maybe a little hurt, but—like Leah—I could tell that you were thinking of me." She laid a hand over his. "How could I be angry with two people so concerned for my happiness?"

A warmth spread through Zeke at her touch... and her words, and he regretted ever doubting her.

THIRTEEN

Rebekah looked around as she stepped down from the buggy. The lake was enormous—so much larger than the pond they had skated on back home. She felt nerves skitter their way up her back as she lifted her old, battered skates out of the buggy.

She looked around the lake and was surprised at what she saw. There were wooden benches set up all around the edge of the lake, two or three every ten feet or so. Behind the benches, there were crates that were turned upside down and she could see boots and shoes resting on several of them.

At least ten feet behind each cluster of benches, there was a table where skaters could get warm cocoa or chili—and she even saw hot dogs at some of them. Beside each table there was a grill or a raised fire pit where the hot cocoa and other were kept warm.

Amazing, she thought. This was clearly something they did a lot and something everyone in the community enjoyed... not just the young people. Looking out over the people assembled she realized there must also be young people from neighboring districts because there were many more young people attending than were in their own district.

"Come on, Rebekah. I see Zeke!" Leah whispered a little too loudly as she grabbed Rebekah's hand and rushed off to join the others.

Rebekah looked back at her *mamm,* who smiled warmly and then turned in Samuel's arms as he laid another warm wrap over her shoulders. He rested his hands on top of her wrap as she leaned back against him.

Rebekah was glad to see them that way. They looked so happy together. Finally she could see how *gut* it was. *Mamm* had not had enough of that in her life.

Dat had been sick for Rebekah's entire life and when he'd died she knew something had happened between *Mamm* and *Onkel* Joel, but she wasn't sure what. And then *Mamm* had come here and met Samuel... and that was clearly *Gotte's* plan for her.

When she realized Leah had stopped pulling on her, she looked around to see what was going on. After only a second, she saw Zeke and felt warmer than she had so far all afternoon. She watched as he dipped his head to her just slightly and she felt a smile tugging at her lips.

She heard a giggle behind her and turned to see Leah and two other young *maedels* watching the exchange with big smiles on their faces. The three of them were just standing there together and smiling, almost as if they were all in on some big, exciting secret.

It was the first time she truly felt like she might have a place here. Rebekah sent a look over her shoulder and was surprised to see that Zeke was still looking right at her. When she looked back, she was greeted by those same three very wide smiles.

"*Allrecht*. Now, let's go get a drink." She linked her arm with Leah's and this time pulled at her. She led her over to the refreshment tables that were set up a fair distance from the shore of the lake.

As they moved toward the table, she thought back to the other *nacht*. Had it all really happened or was it just a dream? She looked over her shoulder and Zeke was standing just where he had been when she noticed him and his eyes had met hers. There was no mistaking the seriousness of his expression.

She smiled at him and then turned back reluctantly so she could see where she was going.

There was a lot of giggling and smiling in her direction as the three *maedels* introduced her to the rest of the young people. She could not help noticing how many families seemed to have as many children as the Fishers.

In Hope Springs, there had been one or two large families, but most of the families had been small. *Mamm* had always wanted to give Rebekah *bruders* and *schweschders,* but *Dat* had been very sick, which made it impossible.

Of course, now I have eleven bruders and schweschders. The irony of it was not lost on her. She had always wished for a bigger family and now she had it... just not the way she expected.

I should be grateful to Gotte. I have so much to be thankful for.

Her thoughts drifted back to the other *nacht.* She thought of how sweetly Zeke had delivered her home. They had talked all the way back to the Fisher *haus.* He had told her of the *haus* he was already building.

"Of course," he had said "I will want your help with it now." and he had laughed at the look of panic that must have appeared on her face.

"Not that kind of help, Rebekah. I mean help with

the planning and arranging. I have no idea of how to go about arranging a kitchen. Even the way to place the rooms are a bit of a mystery to me."

She could remember the rush of heat that had flowed through her at his words. It had spread throughout her body when she thought of the two of them making plans for their future. Without realizing it, she had snuggled into *lieb;* sitting there beside him, with the snow coming down all around them.

"Have you been on the ice yet?" A deep, male voice startled Rebekah and she nearly dropped her hot cocoa.

She took two deep breaths, trying desperately to calm her speeding heart before turning around. She had recognized his voice right away and now she felt a blush creeping up her cheeks. He must have *kumme* to ask her to skate.

"*Nee,* I have not... not yet. We just arrived a few minutes ago."

"Well then, what are you waiting for? Let's go." He held out a hand to her and she put her gloved hand in his bare one. For a moment, she wished she had taken off her gloves. She could feel his hand just a little where her fingers were exposed and she was grateful to *Grossmammi* for knitting her these special gloves.

When she had opened the package last Christmas she had wondered what *Grossmammi* was thinking, giving her gloves that left her fingers exposed to the cold. Then she had seen that there was another part to the gloves—a piece that hinged just above her top knuckles—which was tucked through a special band but could be folded over to cover her fingers.

Grossmammi, you are a genius.

She smiled as the slight brush of his fingers warmed her. She remembered the other *nacht* again and how the gloves had *kumme* in handy with Zeke holding her hand in the buggy on the way home. And she was relieved she had thought to wear the same gloves again today.

Thinking of it made her remember that they would soon know whether or not her grandparents thought Leah's idea of them moving to Windy Gap was a *gut* one. The thought that they might come here to live brought her so much happiness; it almost overshadowed how excited she was to be here with Zeke Hershberger.

Almost...

"Do you need help with your skates?" Although he was speaking quietly, she could clearly hear Zeke's deep voice and she was surprised at how closely he had leaned in to speak to her.

She could feel his breath on her ear and it sent a little chill through her as his question *verhuddelt* her.

What should she do—pretend to need help so that he would have an excuse to hold her feet or tell him she didn't need any help and show him that she was capable?

When she fumbled with her skates and nearly dropped one on his foot, he laughed and the question seemed to answer itself as he took them in his hands and began unlacing them. She felt a blush spread across her cheeks and bent down to unfasten her thick boots in an attempt to hide her flaming face.

"These are *gut* skates. You have skated before, then?"

Rebekah only nodded, partly because she didn't trust her voice and partly because she was overcome with a strong desire to giggle. She tried to concentrate on getting her boots off, but even with the open-fingered gloves, she couldn't get the stiff fasteners to cooperate.

"Let me help you with those." She couldn't tell if Zeke was stifling a laugh or not, but she was grateful that he wasn't laughing at her fumbling attempts.

"*Danki.* I thought these gloves would make it easier but they don't seem to." She sighed, part in frustration, part in acceptance and was surprised when Zeke fumbled a little with her boot. A laugh slipped from her before she could stop it but Zeke joined her and when he looked up at her, she could see he was laughing at himself... not her.

"We both seem to be all thumbs tonight..." And he ended his sentence with a laugh.

Rebekah listened to his deep laughter for a few seconds before joining in. It felt very *gut* to laugh with him. It was especially *gut* to know that they were laughing together, at themselves, and no one was laughing at anyone else.

Their laughter slowed and gradually stopped as he removed her boots and slipped on her skates, tying the laces nice and tight. Then he sat down beside her and slipped his own boots off so that he could put on his own skates.

She couldn't help but notice that his skates were different from most of the other boys. Most of the boys wore the skates used for hockey, Zeke's skates had the sleek, black boot that looked so much like her own.

The blades started with a claw at the front and it looked sharp to her, not worn down like it would be for someone who didn't know how to use it. She wondered at it, but was not certain how to ask him about what that meant.

She also noticed that his skates were in very *gut* condition, clearly not new, but well-taken care of and she wondered at that too, but again, had no notion of how to ask him about it. After he tied the laces up, he stood and held out a hand to her again.

"Are you ready, then?"

"*Jah*, I am." She put her hand in his again and was immediately glad she had not pulled the flap over her fingers. She could not really feel his skin on her palm, but the warmth of his hand came through the thin covering and her fingers felt so warm curled over his hand—she could not imagine getting cold. She smiled up at him as they made their way to the edge of the lake.

She worried that she might lose her balance as she stepped onto the lake with him, but his hand helped steady her and she only wobbled a little as her sharp skates met the thick layers of ice that covered the lake.

He gave her a minute to get her balance and then he pushed off and she tried to follow, amazed at how much easier it was to skate with him than to try and glide along by herself.

"You're doing great." His voice sounded very near her ear again and she nearly lost her balance in surprise, but he held tightly to her and she managed to stay upright. His delighted laughter sounded beside her and she felt a blush creep across her cheeks again.

Will I forever be blushing around him? What will he think of me? Ach, well he's made his choice. Hopefully he will be flattered, thinking that I just can't help myself.

They skated along in quiet for a long time, circling the entire lake several times before Rebekah noticed that even the warmth of his hand was not enough to stop the cold that was seeping slowly into her, starting at her feet.

She wasn't sure what she had done to alert him but it could have been her teeth—no matter how hard she tried, she couldn't seem to keep them from chattering and he was sure to have noticed.

Whatever it was, he gently guided her to the edge of the lake and helped her into the snow again right next to where they had stepped onto the ice. She could see their boots on an overturned crate that was sitting behind the nearest bench.

Rebekah held tightly to Zeke's hand as he helped her to the bench and tried to stop her shivering. For sure and for certain he had noticed it now that he was so much closer to her. Being off the ice only helped a little and she was afraid she was going to embarrass herself when she tried to talk and all that came out was the sound of chattering teeth.

"You stay here. I will be right back." And then he was gone.

Rebekah looked around to see where he had gone,

but there were so many people standing around her, she couldn't spot him so she turned back to her skates and started working on the laces.

She tried untying them, but Zeke had made the knots extra secure and her fingers were freezing, so she tucked the flaps over her fingers and waited, wishing she had thought to do so earlier, while they skated. The cold was somehow more intense on the ice. She'd known that, but at the time she had only been thinking of how *gut* it had felt to have her hand in Zeke's.

"*Ach!* This is impossible." She turned at the laugh that sounded right behind her, just as Zeke draped a blanket over her shoulders.

"It might have helped if I had remembered you are not used to such cold, *jah*?" He knelt in front of her and started undoing the laces that she had given up on.

"*Jah,* it is most certainly colder here than it was in Ohio. I should have known better, too. There is a pond near my grandparent's *haus* that freezes over in winter. The youth skate on it every chance we get. And I should have used the extra flap to cover my fingers." she waved a hand in the air as she said it.

His strong hands deftly unwound the long laces from around the top of her skate and she handed him her boot when he slid her foot out.

"An extra pair of socks would have been a *gut* idea,

too." She laughed as she said it and he joined her.

"Jah, these feet are certainly delicate." He held her boot in his hand a moment before looking up at her with a smile in his eyes.

"I don't think you would have gotten your foot in this boot if you were wearing an extra sock, though."

She giggled at his words. Her boots must look positively tiny to him. Her feet, like her *mamm's,* were a very small size. She had not needed to move up a size in shoes for several years and she saw no reason to think she might anytime soon. Her feet were almost exactly the same size now as *Mamm's,* so they were probably finished growing.

His feet, on the other hand, looked enormous to her. She knew that young men usually kept growing long after young *maedels* had finished, so his feet might have even more growing to do.

"Well isn't that a sight?" The look of surprise on his face as he slid her boot easily onto her foot was comical. No doubt he could see that there was actually room in the boot for another layer of socks, maybe even two.

"Hey! Here you two are... I wondered where you had gone off to." Leah walked over to the bench and dropped down beside Rebekah with a sigh that sounded either exhausted or frustrated—Rebekah couldn't be sure which.

"She insisted I accompany her to the lake so she could skate." Zeke told Leah, and then he winked at her, before turning back to Rebekah, who was watching him and her new *schweschder*.

"Zeke, you shouldn't tease Rebekah. She still doesn't know you like the rest of us. She might think you're serious." She turned to Rebekah and flashed a big smile.

"Besides, I know exactly who it was that came up to the four of us and asked you to go skate." She wiggled her eyebrows a little as she said it. It was all Rebekah could do to suppress her laughter.

Zeke took it completely in stride though, looking up at them with an innocent smile and widening his eyes before he said, "Why Leah Fisher, are you trying to tell me that Rebekah turned some other young man down to skate with me?"

He winked at Rebekah as he said it and she wasn't able to suppress the giggle that time. She covered her mouth quickly with her hand, but that only made her laugh harder. A second later, Zeke and Leah joined her.

She sat there, with an ice skate on one foot and a boot on the other, laughing with her new *schweschder* and a young man she felt certain would be her husband in less than a year. She felt absolutely ecstatic.

Finally, she felt as if she were where she should be.

FOURTEEN

Naomi watched as Rebekah and Leah laughed with young Zeke. She had already asked Samuel about him and he had assured her that Zeke was a fine, young man.

"You know, it's funny," Samuel's voice came from behind her. She didn't turn, knowing he would come near enough to stand right behind her and lend his warmth to her by standing as close as they could get away with.

"I had hoped Zeke was interested in Leah. They have grown up together and he has been to our *haus* more than once to take her to the youth gatherings." He stopped for a moment and she heard a low chuckle before he went on.

"But it appears he is a bit more interested in her new *schweschder*."

Samuel's words surprised her. She had been certain Zeke only skated with Rebekah because he was a nice young man and was trying to make her feel welcome, but looking harder at the group of them, she could see that Samuel was right. Zeke was clearly interested in Rebekah, not Leah.

She took a moment to think about how that made her feel and was surprised to find that there was a little ache around her heart. Her Rebekah was growing up and she had missed so much of it. She started to feel sad, but another thought suddenly interrupted her thoughts.

"*Ach,* Samuel, you don't think this will cause a problem between them, do you? If they like the same boy..." She let her words trail off, but an answer never came. Instead, she heard her name a moment later and turned to find her *aenti* and *onkel* coming toward them.

"Naomi, you're here. *Gut!*" *Aenti* Ida walked up and wrapped Naomi in a warm hug as *Onkel* Ephraim shook Samuel's hand.

"We were hoping you would be here, but we couldn't be certain..." *Aenti* Ida trailed off her words and the look she gave Naomi sent a blush to her cheeks.

"*Aenti* Ida…" Naomi tried to sound shocked, but the laughter coming from Samuel behind her and the wide grin on *Onkel* Ephraim's face was too much for her.

She gave in and joined the laughter. It probably was funny. She and Samuel were not as young as most of the couples who had taken their vows this season but they had certainly enjoyed being newly married.

Even Catherine, who seemed to be more outspoken since becoming David's *frau,* had commented to Naomi that she was happy to see her new father-in-law enjoying *heiraat* so much.

Samuel's voice in her ear surprised her.

"I don't think we have anything to worry about, Naomi. I do not think Leah and Rebekah are interested in the same boy at all."

Naomi looked over again at the three young people and saw that another young man had joined them. He was sitting beside Leah, who had a wide smile on her face. She looked at his face, trying to see if she knew who it was and was surprised to see that it was her cousin, Jacob.

She looked back at Samuel and saw that he was smiling. She smiled in return, but the ache in her heart got a little bigger as she looked back at the two young couples.

The ache was surrounded by warmth and she was

glad to find that she was happy for her two *dochdern,* but she was also a little sad to think that they might be joining the married couples themselves in no time at all.

.   .   .

Leah was surprised when she looked up and saw Jacob walking toward her. She had been looking for him since she stepped down from the buggy and trying hard not to be disappointed that she had not seen him anywhere. Now here he was walking right to her.

She felt heat flood her cheeks and looked down at the ground for a moment to try and get control of the giggles that were trying to escape. When she looked up again, he was standing right in front of her with a big smile on his face.

"I was worried I wouldn't be able to find you, but here you are. Have you been on the ice yet?"

"I have, but I wouldn't mind another turn." She ducked her head when she felt another giggle trying to escape.

He took her hand and pulled her along with him over to an empty spot on the long, wooden bench. She looked down at their joined hands and then up to his face.

"Do you mind?" All she could do was shake her head back and forth as a little thrill rushed through her. She was so *eiferich;* this must mean he was ready to announce their relationship.

"*Jah,* Leah." he said with a laugh as he gently tapped the end of her nose with his finger. "I can see the wheels turning in that head of yours. We have an entire year to wait, but I don't want us to hide anymore."

"Oh, Jacob, that is wonderful." She smiled up at him as he settled her on the bench and sat down beside her.

Her skates were already on, so she sat and watched Jacob put his on, then lace them up tightly. It must have taken him twice as long as it should have because he kept looking up at her or reaching over to squeeze her hand—the entire time.

Once his skates were fastened, he took her hand and they moved to the edge of the ice together. She couldn't help feeling like they were the only two people here; everyone else had disappeared from her notice.

She did not even feel the cold as they skated along in a smooth rhythm and she took a moment to be thankful she had been skating on this pond her entire life.

. . .

Back on the shore, Zeke was gently rubbing Rebekah's hands, trying to restore some of the warmth, when Jacob and Leah skated past them.

"I guess they're finished hiding their relationship." he looked over at Rebekah as he spoke and he laughed a little. "I think perhaps we are, too." and at Rebekah's questioning look, he nodded behind her.

She turned to follow the direction he was looking and met her *mamm's* gaze. Samuel was standing beside her, talking to one of the men from the district whose name she could not remember, but she knew he was a friend of Samuel's.

Rebekah waited to see how *Mamm* would react.

Is she angry with me for keeping this a secret? Will she be disappointed in my choice?

Rebekah thought she could see a hint of sadness in her *mamm's* face, but then her smile bloomed and it was clear that she was happy for her *dochder*. Rebekah felt herself relax little by little, a smile spreading across her own features.

She realized then, that she felt warmer than she had been all evening. She knew now would be the best time to officially introduce Zeke to *Mamm* and Samuel— even though they already knew each other.

She looked up at Zeke with a clear question in her

expression. He didn't hesitate, as if he knew exactly what she was asking him.

"*Kumme,* then. Let's go make this official, *jah.*" He patted her boots to make certain they were secure before standing up, dusting himself off and taking her hand to gently pull her up from the bench.

Together they walked across the long expanse of snowy yard between them and her *mamm* and step *dat.* She felt *gelassenheit* settle over her as they moved closer. Zeke's hand was warm and comforting, wrapped around hers.

Samuel and his friend must have noticed them approaching because the other man said something to Samuel and then smiled over at the two of them, before drifting away and walking back toward the lake.

Samuel smiled as they got closer. As soon as they were close enough, he held out a hand to Zeke. When Zeke took the offered hand, Samuel pulled him closer, clapping him on the back with his other hand and Rebekah relaxed even more.

"I can see now that I was pushing the wrong *schweschder.*" Samuel said with a laugh, before releasing Zeke.

As Zeke stepped back, he laughed with Samuel. Then he slipped his arm around Rebekah and hugged her to his side.

"*Jah,* it does look that way." He looked down at Rebekah and the emotion on his face was clear enough, she was certain everyone who saw him would know exactly what he was thinking. "We never know what *Gotte* has in mind for us, ain't so?"

Samuel laughed again as he mirrored Zeke's stance, slipping his arm around Naomi. "I never expected what *Gotte* had in mind for me with Naomi, but He knows what is best for us, for sure and for certain."

"*Jah,* He does." Zeke looked down at Rebekah and his arm tightened around her shoulders as he answered Samuel.

Rebekah looked at *Mamm...* She thought she could see sadness in *Mamm's* expression, but before she could be certain, a smile had spread across the face that had tilted up to look at Samuel. The emotion on *Mamm's* face now was clear.

Mamm might be *bedauerlich* to think that her *dochder* would soon be grown up, married and gone—but she would not be alone.

FIFTEEN

Rebekah looked up at Zeke as he drove the buggy. It seemed to her that he had just made his intentions known to Samuel and her *mamm*... but there was still a niggling doubt in the back of Rebekah's mind.

Zeke looked over at her then and there was such a look of tenderness, plus one of deep emotion that she had yet to completely identify, that she felt better at once.

Could he be in lieb with me already? We have only known each other a week... I wish I could know for certain how he feels about me.

"Do you think we will get there before Jacob and

Leah this time?" Zeke asked with a laugh. Rebekah felt herself laughing in answer.

"I would not count on it." After another minute, she added, "Do you think Samuel was more surprised by our announcement or by Leah and Jacob's?"

Zeke didn't say anything about her calling Samuel by his name, but he did give her a slightly *schpassich* look. "I think we all took him by surprise."

Rebekah giggled at the memory of Samuel's face when Jacob and Leah told him of their plans. Seeing the two of them together at the skating party, Samuel had to suspect they were courting, but he clearly had not expected Jacob to approach him that same night and ask for permission to marry Leah in the fall.

She looked over at Zeke as he drove the team. She watched his hands as he held the reins. He was so sure of himself and she could not help but wonder... would they be making the same announcement next year?

She turned her head at the sudden blush that filled her cheeks with color and heat. It was much too soon to be thinking things like that. They had only been together a handful of times and never truly alone, except for their time traveling in the buggy.

She was comforted though, to think that they no longer had to hide their courting from *Mamm* and Samuel. Zeke could simply pick her up and take her for a ride. She was excited to realize that he could *kumme* for dinner some evening soon. It would be so *gut* to watch him with her new family. She found herself laughing at the thought that followed.

Zeke looked over at her and she tried to slow her laughter so she could explain, but ended up waving a hand to him in defeat. He looked back at the road and then back over to her before she was finally able to get control of herself and tell him what was tickling her so.

"Sorry, Zeke. I was just thinking about how exciting it will be to invite you to dinner, and..." a giggle interrupted her words and it took another second before she was able to continue, "... it suddenly occurred to me that you have known my new family much longer than I have."

Zeke looked at her for several seconds before he began laughing along with her. They laughed together for several seconds before the mood began to pass.

Rebekah looked over at Zeke as his laughter slowed. Now that she could think about the situation and not worry about there being anything between Leah and Zeke, perhaps it would be to her advantage that Zeke was better acquainted with her new family. He could give her insights about things she wouldn't want to ask Leah, and he would have a different perspective on the family dynamics as a friend.

She smiled when he looked over at her and she felt some of the tension she had been feeling since moving here ease. It was a relief to discover there was something for her in Windy Gap... *or rather someone.*

With all the craziness in that haus, it is so nice to find some calm exists here after all. If Zeke can give me some pointers, it just might make living with so much chaos a little easier.

"And how are you getting on with your new family?" Zeke's voice interrupted her thoughts and she was surprised at his question.

It was as if he had been reading her thoughts again. She tried to think of something to say in return, but no words would form.

"I can see the wheels turning in that head of yours, Rebekah. I would guess that you are having a hard time adjusting to the chaos, but you don't want to say anything negative about the Fisher family." He stopped, and then a moment later added, "Am I right?" and she could only nod.

"They can be overwhelming. I have been friends with Caleb and Elam since we were in school together and I have spent many a *nacht* at their dinner table over the years. Even in their grief, they were always an..." He paused a moment and she could see he was searching for the right word. It was several seconds before he went on and when he did, a slightly mischievous smile spread across his face. "...energetic family."

She laughed at that. "*Jah,* they do seem to possess more energy than most families I know. And there are so many of them." She shook her head as she went on. "Even Caleb, who really should be resting, has so much energy he just cannot keep still. His *bruders* have brought him all manner of harnesses and leather things which he is mending while he's required to stay off his leg."

"That," Zeke said pointedly, "does not surprise me at all. Caleb was always the one who seemed to get in the most trouble in the classroom. The energy within him would just spill out, at the oddest of times, and before we knew it he would be in trouble--again." After a moment he added, "Though at times it was quite entertaining." He laughed as he said it, as if he were remembering something specific.

Rebekah just sat there, watching him as he reminisced. It was *gut* to see him like this. So much of her life had been filled with sadness or exhaustion. She could not remember many times at all when her *dat* had been excited and full of life.

He had done everything possible to remain *gelassenheit* and happy even until the very end—but never with much energy. There had always been an oppressing air of exhaustion that hung in the *haus*.

It was one of the reasons she had spent so much time with her grandparents. Even though her *grossmammi* had often been tired, there was not such an oppression about it. She was simply tired because she worked hard to keep their little *haus* clean, to cook for all of them, and to help out in the community.

Grossdaddi was another matter. He had always had an energy that was infectious. Just being around him had always made Rebekah feel as if she had more energy, too—so it was no secret that she enjoyed being with him.

In a few ways, Zeke reminded her of *Grossdaddi*—not in the way of his energy, but in how animated and excited he would become when speaking of certain subjects. She could tell that the Fisher family was important to him. And thinking about that made her realize how little she knew about his own family. That would need to be remedied.

"Zeke..." she waited a moment before going on—and as she waited he looked at her expectantly. She gathered her courage and plunged on, "I can tell that the Fisher family is very important to you. You talk about them an awful lot. But you never talk about your own family. Will you tell me about them?"

He let out a breath that was at least half laughter before answering. "*Ach.* That is not at all what I was expecting you to ask."

She didn't ask—but she wanted to—what he had thought she was going to say.

Perhaps later... for now, she sat quietly and listened to him.

"My family is much like the Fisher family—only it was my *dat* we lost. I never even knew him. He died two months before I was born, and *Mamm* named me for him." he stopped there for a moment and Rebekah sat there thinking about his words.

She could not help wondering what her own life would have been like if she'd never known her *dat*. He may not have been able to do what other *dats* could but he had loved her—of that much she was certain. And she had spent a great deal of time following him around on their farm when she was younger and he was still able to work the fields.

He had taught her so many things—and now she could see that that was truly what she missed most. It had felt as if she'd lost him when his disease had taken those times away from her. She knew then that she would never trade what little time she'd had with her own *dat* to have lived even minute without a *dat* in her life. She placed a hand on Zeke's arm and when he looked at her, she was certain she could see his pain reflected in his eyes—swirling within the depths—just as her own had been for so long.

"I am genuinely sorry, Zeke. I didn't know."

He opened his mouth to speak, but closed it immediately and gave his head a little shake before opening it again.

"I was going to say it's allrecht, but if I'm being honest with myself—" and he looked over at her again, "and with you, I have to admit that it has never been allrecht."

"I suppose I latched onto the Fisher family because Caleb and Elam let me. We knew each other in school, *jah,* but I often spent more time at their *haus* when I was a young man than I did at my own." He rubbed a restless hand over his face before continuing.

"I am the youngest of seven *bruders*... well, eight actually, but my *bruder* Silas died when he was only twelve. I never knew him, either." He looked over at her again and she was surprised to see him steering the buggy off the road.

Ach. Jacob and Leah will forever be thinking we are stopping off to spark on our way to meet them. And she put a hand to her mouth to stop the giggle that was threatening to burst from her lips—this was not the time for laughter.

Zeke turned back to her and she forced herself to put on a serious face to match the subject they had been discussing before she was distracted by her own errant thought. She was able to drop her hand just before Zeke looked at her.

"The truth is I have never truly felt as if I fit in my family. My closest *bruder* is six years older than me. None of us have seen or heard from him in five years; not since he decided to leave the community."

It was all Rebekah could do to smother the shock she felt. She had never known anyone who had jumped the fence, but she knew of a family in Hope Springs whose *dochder* had done it. It had been very difficult on them. Their younger *dochder* had been in school with Rebekah and things had seemed to be especially rough for her after that. It was as if her parents thought they could make Sarah stay if they just held on tight enough. Rebekah could not imagine how difficult it must be for Zeke—especially being the youngest.

"With the Fisher family, I felt as if I fit in. I suppose it is not such a surprise that Samuel expected me to feel differently toward Leah." He shook his head a little but went on. "If I had not felt the need to please Samuel, I might have realized earlier that I feel like Leah is my little *schweschder*." He laughed then.

"She knew. All along, she knew I felt more like a

bruder to her than a potential beau. I am sure she only rode to that singing with me to make her *dat* happy." He looked down at the reins in his hands and was silent for what felt like a long time.

"I suppose that is why I feel the way I do about kissing." He was silent again and Rebekah thought about his words—hoping he would explain. Thankfully, before her curiosity got the best of her, he did.

"My *bruder* Seth married so quickly after *Dat* died. It took a long time before I saw it—and *Mamm* never said anything—but I finally did see it for myself." He stopped again and it looked as if he were gathering his courage. Whatever he was about to say must be a difficult thing and Rebekah couldn't help herself... her curiosity was positively burning now.

All she knew about his *bruder* Seth was that he lived in Ohio with his *frau*. Rebekah was opening her mouth to ask Zeke what he'd finally seen, when he answered her.

"He did not marry for love. Reba had lost her entire family and we had just lost *Dat* and they knew each other from school and they thought it would be a *gut* idea. *Mamm* was grieving so heavily herself that she must have missed seeing how they truly felt about each other." His words confused Rebekah.

She knew that happened quite often. Lots of people

in the community married for convenience... *didn't they?* Wasn't that was *Onkel* Joel had expected of *Mamm* after *Dat* died?

Of course, Mamm had other ideas about that...

"But—" Before she could say more, he began speaking again.

"When I was twelve, Reba came back." When he said those words, he hung his head and it looked as if the weight of the world was on his shoulders.

Rebekah reached over and placed a hand on his back, trying to find some way to help him. She still did not quite understand what he was talking about, so she sat there, gently rubbing her hand along his back, trying to help in the only way she could think of.

It was nearly a minute before Zeke spoke again. "It only took them two years to be sick of each other and Reba only stayed for a year after that before she decided she couldn't live like that anymore." And with those words, Rebekah began to understand. Seth's *frau* had left the community; she had left her husband.

When she spoke, her voice was so low, she wasn't even certain Zeke could hear her. "And you were twelve before she came back?"

Zeke nodded and took a deep breath before continuing. "Nearly ten years she stayed away before she decided to *kumme* back and give my *bruder* another chance."

"Did they have any *kinner?*" Rebekah asked, not entirely certain she wanted to know the answer.

"*Nae.* They still have none, actually. I think that may have had something to do with her leaving, but I can't be certain. Seth has never spoken of this to me. It was only by listening to *Mamm* read his letters that I began to realize what was going on."

"Seth and Reba moved to Ohio when I was not quite two. I do not even think *Mamm* knew they were having troubles then. Seth was offered a *gut* job with *Mamm's* cousin and I suppose they thought a change would do them *gut.*"

"But..." Rebekah prompted softly, again not certain she really wanted to know.

"Reba cannot have *kinner.* When she left, I was much too young to know anything about what was going on. And even as I got older, it didn't truly sink in until she came back. *Mamm* finally began to smile again after that."

He turned to her then and took both of her hands in his. "You understand, don't you, Rebekah? I wanted to make certain that I would choose someone for the right reasons. I did not want to go through what my *bruder* has."

Rebekah was nodding before he finished speaking.

"Of course I understand, Zeke. It makes perfect sense to me." she ducked her head a little before she went on. "I thought it was a wonderful idea to begin with."

Zeke didn't say anything else. After a few moments, Rebekah started to fret, so she looked up at him. It was such a relief to see the smile that had spread across his face. She let out the breath she hadn't even realized she was holding and felt a tremendous weight lift off her shoulders.

"How do you feel about hugs?" Zeke asked her then.

"I'm all in favor of them." She barely got the words out of her mouth before Zeke pulled her against his chest and held her there.

She snuggled into his warmth and felt more content than she could remember feeling in a very long time. This was most certainly where she was meant to be.

It was several minutes before they pulled apart. Rebekah almost resisted Zeke's gentle withdrawal. Now that she had found such happiness, she didn't want to give up even a moment of it.

"We had better get to the *kaffe* shop. What will Jacob and Leah think?" Zeke said, even as he began laughing.

He picked up the reins and started to signal the team when a loud noise came from outside and distracted them both. Rebekah jumped at the loud music that was pounding through the closed windows of the car that roared past them, going entirely too fast for the dark, country road.

Zeke laid a hand over hers before turning to speak softly to the team, trying to settle them before he directed them back onto the road. She was relieved to see him carefully check both ways before pulling the buggy back onto the road. She took a moment to pray silently for Jacob and Leah... or any other buggies that might be on the road with that car.

SIXTEEN

Zeke breathed a sigh of relief when they arrived in the special parking lot beside Higher Grounds and saw Jacob's courting buggy already there. He stepped down and went around to help Rebekah down.

He had just reached for her hand when Jacob came out of the *kaffe* shop with Leah right behind him. Both their faces held anxious looks as they rushed across the small street that separated the shop from the parking lot.

"Zeke!" Jacob was nearly shouting, calling to his *freind* before he had even crossed the street. "*Ach!* I'm so glad we found you."

"We were worried." Leah added, looking in Rebekah's direction.

"You can stop worrying. We are just fine." Zeke answered, but Jacob was shaking his head before Zeke finished.

"It is *gut* you are fine, but we cannot stop worrying." he stopped just a moment as the sound of tires on gravel drowned out his words. Zeke looked over to see a large van pulling into the parking lot beside them.

It only took a moment to recognize the man behind the wheel—but what was their neighbor doing here so late? Zeke knew Phil did not drink *kaffe.* For some reason Jacob's words came back to him then. Why did he say they still had a reason to worry? Quickly he turned to Jacob for an explanation.

"Zeke, your *Mamm* is in the hospital." Jacob put a hand on his shoulder and squeezed, but Zeke hardly felt it. *Mamm* was in the hospital... Why? How? There were so many questions flooding his thoughts, but he couldn't seem to make his voice work. He just stood there looking at Jacob, hoping hoping his *freind* would have an answer to some of them.

"I'm sorry to have to be the one to tell you and I wish it was not this way." Jacob continued. "She was on her way home from the skating party and a car ran her off the road." Jacob stopped for a moment and took a deep breath before going on.

Ach! The news must be really bad if he is having this much difficulty telling me. The words ran through Zeke's head just before Jacob spoke again.

"It would not have been so bad if she had stopped at the edge of the road..." another bracing breath and Jacob went on. "but the car struck so hard that her buggy rolled several times. They would not tell Miranda much because she is not family, but they did say that she needed to find the family as quickly as she could and get them to the hospital." He waved a hand in Phil's direction.

"It was a blessing indeed that Phil was on his way home and saw the whole thing. He used that fancy cell phone of his and got the ambulance there quick." Jacob nodded in Phil's direction and Zeke looked over at Phil, trying to put a look of gratefulness on his face, but his features felt like they were frozen. Phil was nodding at him though. Zeke hoped his neighbor knew what Zeke wanted to say.

"Zeke, I know this has all been a shock to you, but we really should get going. Most of the family is already there." Phil's voice was full of concern. Zeke shook his head a little and turned to Rebekah. He wanted to ask her to *kumme* with him to the hospital, but he wasn't sure it was proper or a *gut* idea. Who knew how long he would be there and it was already quite late.

Fortunately, Jacob had the solution to that problem as well. He spoke before Zeke could open his mouth.

"I called the Fishers... I hope you don't mind. Benjamin happened to be at the shanty and answered the phone, so I told him what was going on. Leah agreed that we should be there with you. You will need friends as well as family now."

Zeke looked back to Rebekah's face as Jacob explained and felt some of the tension leave him when he saw how relieved she was to hear that she would be going with him to the hospital. And with that, he wasted no more time.

Knowing that he was in no shape to be much company, he opted for the back seat of the van, so he opened the side door and made his way to the back, sliding across the long bench and pulling Rebekah with him. Then he waited while Jacob and Leah settled themselves in the middle seat and closed the door before he reached up to lay a hand on Jacob's shoulder.

"*Danki,* Jacob. You have no idea what this means to me."

Jacob nodded his head as he answered. "*Jah,* I do. It is no less than you would do for me." Zeke turned to Rebekah.

"*Danki.*" He wanted to say more, but the words wouldn't *kumme.*

Not that it mattered. Rebekah sat quietly beside him, holding onto his hand, trying to bring him comfort. She held on all the way to the hospital—even when she bowed her head to pray silently, she kept holding tightly to his hand. Something about her small, delicate hands holding so tightly to his large, calloused hand made him keep his attention focused on that... on her... and he forgot to worry nearly all the way there.

Only when they turned into the well-lit parking area of the hospital and Phil wound his way around to the back side of the building—where the emergency room was located—did Zeke begin to worry again.

He was grateful that Jacob was much more in control than he was. The calm, young man he was beginning to consider a *gut* friend led them all through the doors that swished open and shut with barely a sound and into a large, waiting area that seemed to be overly full of people. Everywhere Zeke looked he could see crowds of people.

Fortunately, he saw his *bruders* fairly quickly. They were standing with a man in a long, white coat, conversing in low voices. Simon was standing next to the man Zeke could only guess was the doctor, nodding as the man spoke. Timothy was on the man's other side, shifting from foot to foot and looking more uncomfortable by the second. Thomas was standing beside Simon, listening intently as his young *frau* Cora leaned against him, silent tears making their way down her cheeks.

With Rebekah's hand tucked firmly in his own, Zeke squared his shoulders and made his way over to the group. He caught a few words as they got closer, but none of them made any sense to him. He could only hope that someone would explain to him what was going on.

When he reached the small circle made by his *bruders* and the doctor, Timothy turned to him. It only took a second for his *bruder* to engulf Zeke in a tight hug. Timothy had always been the most demonstrative of them and Zeke was not at all surprised at the reaction. Over Timothy's shoulders, Zeke noticed Simon's raised eyebrows and was certain it was due to how tightly Zeke was holding onto Rebekah, but he would deal with that later.

The man in the white coat turned to Zeke and Rebekah just as Timothy loosened his grip and stepped back. He reached out a hand and then surprised Zeke by placing it on Zeke's shoulder and giving it a light squeeze.

"You must be Zeke," and he went on as Zeke

nodded. "Your brothers have been quite worried about you. I'm glad they were able to locate you so quickly." He gestured to the side and behind him as he spoke.

"I was just going over your mother's injuries and our treatment plan." He stopped for a moment and when Zeke said nothing, he went on. "Her condition is stable for the moment, but I am very concerned. In fact, it's a miracle she is still with us."

Zeke wasn't sure how to take the man's words. It sounded like *gut* news, but it also sounded as if there was a chance things could be bad, too.

"If the buggy had stopped after just rolling over once, she most likely would have had only a few bruises and a slight concussion—perhaps a broken bone or two. But it did not roll just the one time and that has left us with a great deal more injuries and a very serious concussion." He looked around at the group before continuing.

"We have scheduled surgery first thing in the morning to deal with the worst of the breaks. We set the ones we were able to, but I am particularly concerned about two bones in her left leg. On the x-ray, they appeared to be shattered but an ultrasound has shown us that is not the case. They are both broken in several places and will require surgery to set them correctly." Thomas had leaned forward like he had a question and when the doctor stopped talking, he spoke up.

"Will we be able to see her soon? Talk to her?" But before he even finished, the doctor was shaking his head.

"She is heavily sedated at the moment. We don't want her to move or thrash about and make any of the breaks worse—and of course, we don't want her to be in any additional pain." He looked around at us and then added, "Of course, you are welcome to come in and *see* her. As long as you understand—she won't be awake and you really shouldn't touch her right now."

Timothy spoke up again. "I would at least like to see her, and have the opportunity to pray over her." He looked up at each of his brothers in turn.

Zeke found himself nodding. "I would like the chance to see *Mamm* as well." Knowing she was hurt so seriously was unnerving enough without waiting until some point tomorrow to even see her.

When Thomas and Simon nodded as well, the doctor must have realized he would not be able to convince them otherwise so he gave in.

"All right, then. Follow me, please." Then he turned toward a set of double doors Zeke hadn't even noticed before.

When he stepped up to them, he nodded to a nurse

who was sitting behind a long counter near the doors. A strange buzz sounded and the doors swung open on their own. The doctor was moving through them before they even opened all the way. Quickly Zeke and his brothers followed him.

It was only when they had left the waiting area that Zeke realized Rebekah's hand was still held tightly in his own. No one had said anything about her coming or not, so he kept hold of her and followed the doctor's quick steps. It was surprisingly comforting to feel Rebekah's tiny fingers in his own.

SEVENTEEN

Rebekah turned to look back at Leah as she and Zeke moved toward the double doors that swooshed open with barely a sound. Leah shrugged her shoulders, but was otherwise unhelpful.

She had a strange feeling that she was not really supposed to be there, but Zeke had quite a grip on her hand and she really didn't want to pull away from him when he clearly needed her, so she followed and tried to stay as quiet as possible, hoping no one would notice her and send her away—likely upsetting Zeke in the process.

As they moved quickly through a maze of hallways that all looked the same, she thought over what the doctor had said. Zeke's *Mamm* would need surgery to set the bones in her leg and she had several other broken bones. She was heavily sedated, but she also had a concussion. It sounded very frightening. But at the same time, Rebekah could remember hearing hope in the doctor's kind voice. That had to mean something, didn't it?

Surely he wouldn't give Zeke and his bruders hope unless there truly was some... would he?

If she was completely honest with herself though, she knew he might. She could remember times when doctors had told *Mamm* that a new medication they wanted *Dat* to try had shown amazing results in others. Perhaps they had not meant to give them false hope, but they sure enough had and Rebekah had to wonder if that could be what was happening here as well.

Rebekah was determined, either way—to be nothing but supportive for Zeke. If the doctor was giving them false hope, he would surely need it to get through this ordeal. If he was not, Zeke would certainly just appreciate her being here for him. That must be why he had kept such a tight hold to her hand from the moment they stepped out of the van.

As she followed along, Rebekah was momentarily distracted when she saw that the doctor had moved through another set of double doors and into another part of the hospital. This felt more like a normal hallway and she wondered how Reba could possibly be well enough to be in a regular room.

No more than a moment later, the doctor stepped up to an elevator and pressed the button to go up. Beside the elevator doors, there was a sign that told where the elevator went. As she scanned the names, she realized that this particular elevator did not go to any of the regular patient rooms. Wherever he was taking them, this elevator was meant to reach areas where they kept the people who were in need of extra care.

Rebekah could still remember the times *Dat* had been in the intensive care unit of the hospital back home. It had always infuriated her that she was not allowed to visit him, but they'd had strict rules about who was allowed to visit—and when—and children had not been allowed at any time.

The only *gut* thing about those times were the memories she had of sitting with her grandparents while *Mamm* visited with *Dat*.

They would kumme to the hospital to sit with me. We would play games and talk. Even though I had been hurt that Mamm was allowed in to see Dat and I was not, I had always known that at least I could enjoy my grandparents' company.

The ding of the elevator bell pulled Rebekah from her thoughts and she looked to see which button the doctor would push. For certain, he pushed the button for the floor that had said ICU on the sign. Reba's condition must be very serious indeed. Zeke would need all the strength Rebekah could give him.

In that moment, she realized that she was glad for all of the times she had put forth a strength for *Mamm*--strength that she had not known she had within her. Her *mamm* had needed all of the strength Rebekah could muster for her and now that experience could help her to be strong for Jake and his *bruders*.

She looked up when the doors opened. Right away she could see the similarities. This hospital was laid out much the same as the one back home. Directly in front of the elevators was a long counter. Behind that counter sat a nurse who was typing away furiously at something.

At each side of the counter, a hall stretched out and around—making a half circle. Rooms lined the outer edges of the halls, but they were different from regular rooms. Each room had a glass door and large glass panels instead of walls.

When Rebekah had first seen an Intensive Care Unit, it had been different, but the second time she could remember *Dat* being in the ICU, the rooms had been changed to look the same as the ones she was seeing now.

The nurse never looked up from her typing. The doctor moved behind the counter to pick up a chart, hopefully Reba Hershberger's and not one for another patient. Timothy looked like he wanted to follow the doctor when he moved behind the counter, but his indecision lasted only a moment, before he leaned back on his heels and waited with the rest of his *bruders*.

It was then that Rebekah noticed Cora. She was crying silently against Thomas' shoulder and wasn't paying any attention to anyone around her. Rebekah wondered if she would do the same if Reba was already her mother-in-law.

The thought of how *wunderbaar* it would feel to be a part of Zeke's family was nearly enough to distract her from what was going on around her... nearly.

Whether I am to be or not one day, I am here right now, just as if I am.

With that in mind, Rebekah squeezed the hand that held hers—and when Zeke looked over at her, she leaned into him a little, trying to do what she could without speaking to lend him her support and strength.

After another moment, the doctor came back from behind the counter carrying what must be Reba's chart. He moved around the long stretch of counter and headed over to the little group without ever looking up.

"Well, there's nothing new here." He looked up, glancing at each *bruder* before speaking again. "Are you certain you wish to see her? She isn't going to look like herself at all and sometimes—" He stopped there a moment. "Well, the wires and machines tend to upset family members."

Rebekah couldn't help but notice that he was looking at Timothy when he said this. What could that mean? No one else seemed to notice and the Hershberger *bruders* were clearly not willing to move before they saw their *mamm*. The doctor must have noticed their resolve, because he nodded his head once, walked over to replace the chart and then moved back around the counter and headed down the hall to the right.

Everyone followed him. Rebekah felt Zeke squeeze her hand again. When she looked up at him, he was watching her with a serious expression on his face. The depth of emotion in his eyes was impossible to miss. It was all she could do to contain the tears that were suddenly clouding her vision. She trusted Zeke to lead her while she worked to clear her vision.

When several tears sneaked past her furious blinking, Rebekah swiped a hand across her face quickly—and nearly collided with Zeke when he came to an abrupt stop.

It took a moment for her to focus on what had stopped Zeke, but it only took a moment to realize they had stopped at the threshold of the small room. Zeke stood in the large, open doorway, while his *bruders* made their way into the room to gather around the bed that stood in the middle of the far wall, where numerous machines were running.

The sight on the bed must have been what stopped him. Reba Hershberger laid there, covered in stark, white bandages and hooked up to all manner of tubes and wires. She looked nothing like the vibrant woman Rebekah had met earlier this evening. She looked small and frail in the enormous bed, covered with many foreign objects and with no prayer covering on her head.

For some reason, the thought came to Rebekah that at leat they had her covered modestly. Rebekah wasn't certain where that thought came from, except that she knew it would be even harder on Zeke and his *bruders* if they had to deal with their *mamm's* modesty being compromised right in front of them.

Zeke was no longer just holding Rebekah's hand. There was an urgency in his fingers—almost as if he was clinging to her hand.

He can't be taking this very well. I for sure don't

blame him, but I have no idea what to do for him, except to stay by his side as long as he needs me there.

With no other ideas coming to mind, Rebekah dropped her head a bit and began praying. She prayed for Reba Hershberger, and for her sons, and for the rest of her family. She prayed that *Gotte* would keep a hand on this wonderful woman who had been so welcoming to her earlier this evening. She prayed for the doctors who were caring for her. She didn't know what else to pray, but no one was moving and when she looked around, she could see that Simon and Thomas were praying, too.

Cora was still crying, but she looked as if she was also praying. Timothy was standing next to his *mamm* with one hand stretched out, almost as if he wanted to touch her, but was clearly afraid he would hurt her if he did.

Rebekah could see why. What little bit of skin they could see that was not covered by bandages, was covered in deep, purple bruises. Silently, she began to pray for Zeke's *mamm*.

·   ·   ·

"The doctor says she needs to go south. *Mamm* says we have family in Pinecraft, but I don't much remember when we last visited." Simon was pacing slowly from the outer wall of the living room to the entry hall as he spoke, the heels of his boots making a hard, loud, thump with each step.

Zeke thought about what the doctor had told them this afternoon. *Mamm* needed to be somewhere warm to properly recover. With the arthritis that already plagued her, he worried that her broken bones would not heal properly unless a warmer climate took the pressure off her joints.

And now he was sitting here, watching Simon pace back and forth as he tried to figure out how to work it all out. Zeke had a strong feeling that he knew what was coming, but he was trying hard to stop thinking about it—just in case Simon could read the thought in his eyes.

They might be able to convince Seth or Stephen to move south but their *kinner* were nowhere near old enough to take over their farms and it simply would not do for them to ask either *bruder* to just leave their farm for who knew how long.

Simon, Timothy and Thomas had similar responsibilities here in Windy Gap, which left only Zeke and Tobias—and since no one in the family knew where Tobias was, that left Zeke. Since he was not married yet and he had only his side business of building furniture, he was the only *bruder* who could pick up and move to Florida with *Mamm*.

No one had specifically asked him, but he knew as well as they did that it was the only option that made any sense. And, as much as he did not want to leave Windy Gap—and Rebekah—he knew it was the right thing to do. Making furniture was something he could do anywhere.

Not that I will have much time for that while I am taking care of Mamm. He knew the time would *kumme* for him to tell his *bruders* that he would be the one to go, but for the moment, he could only think of one thing.

Dear Gott, help me to do this. I know tis the right thing. But if I must go, give me the strength to go—and to leave Rebekah. Ach! What about Rebekah... how will I tell Rebekah?

As he prayed, thoughts went round and round in his head but no answer came.

.   .   .

Rebekah stood at the sink, stirring dough in a large, mixing bowl and staring out the window that looked out over the side yard. Matthew was running around the yard chasing his dog, whose name she could never remember, while Leah pulled laundry from the line.

Rebekah had to smile because Leah wore a nearly identical smile to her own. Clearly she was feeling just as loving toward Jacob as Rebekah was to Zeke.

Who would have thought... only a month ago, I could hardly wait to get back to Ohio. The idea came suddenly but instead of feeling concern, she felt such clarity. She was finally where *Gotte* wanted her.

She had a wonderful family, *bruders* and *schweschders,* and an amazing young man who had already made it clear that he meant to marry her.

The man who had hit his *mamm* had been arrested and would pose no more danger for some time. And Reba Hershberger was already recovering from her injuries. It was true she would have a long road ahead of her, but *Gotte* had truly been watching over her that *nacht.*

Life could not get any better.

Rebekah felt her smile widen when, with no warning at all, Lillian popped up beside her and peered into the large bowl in her hands.

"What are you making?"

"Well..." Rebekah tucked her tongue in her cheek and watched as Lillian practically bounced in anticipation. "It looks like cookie dough to me." She smiled as Lillian huffed at her.

"What kind of cookie dough?"

Rebekah smiled again at the exasperation in the young voice. Lillian was so close to being a teenager and this was clearly a time when she was feeling impatient with her adolescence.

"I was thinking of making double chocolate cookies." She did not add that she was making them because Leah had told her they were Zeke's favorite.

It was bad enough that Leah knew how she felt about Zeke. It would not do to have everyone jumping in with advice and suggestions—not yet anyway. Zeke may have made his intentions clear to *Mamm* and Samuel, but that did not mean he was ready to announce their relationship to the entire district, and telling the younger *kinner* in the family would essentially be doing just that.

"Can I help?" Lillian looked around—probably at the mess Rebekah had made in the kitchen. Even with helping Leah as often as she had been, she'd not yet learned where everything was, so she had pulled a few extra things out of the cabinets in her search for all of the ingredients she would need.

"Of course you can help, Lillian." She started to ask if Lillian would mind helping her find the cookie sheets, but when she turned, Lillian was just turning away from a cabinet by the stove, pans in hand.

"Lillian, you read my mind!" She laughed as she said it and Lillian joined in immediately.

"Well, it was rather obvious what you would need next." Lillian turned and headed over to the table, where she proceeded to lay them out on the table, ready to be filled with cookie dough.

EIGHTEEN

"I can't do it Rebekah. I just can't" Zeke wrapped his arms around her and pulled her as close to him as he could.

She turned her head and leaned into him, trying to turn off the tears that seemed to be on full-force, no matter what she did. It was a tragedy, for sure and for certain, but what was she to do? She could not go and he could not stay.

"Ask me to stay, I am begging you." His words broke her heart, but Rebekah knew it would not be the right thing to do even as he asked so she shook her head, turning her face against his chest as she tried to muffle her sobs.

"I can't leave you."

"But you have to, Zeke. Your *Mamm* can't do this alone and you would not want her to." They were the most difficult words she had ever spoken, but she knew they had to be said.

"You have to go. You know you do." She tried to pull away, even though it felt like her heart was breaking in two, but he wouldn't let her go. His strong arms held her in place against his chest.

They stood like that for what felt like a long time, but when Zeke finally let go, he did so very slowly and Rebekah could feel that it was a struggle for him, certainly as much as it was for her to step away from him. He didn't let her go completely though, he held her at arms length and waited until she looked up at him through her tears before speaking again.

"I'll write to you every day." he said, still holding tightly to her hands.

"That is silly, Zeke." Rebekah was momentarily distracted by his words. There were not enough hours in the day for the things he already must do. She certainly did not want him spending time writing to her —when he could be doing something else.

"You won't have time to write every single day. Once a week is surely enough. You're going to have a lot to do, with taking care of your *mamm* and getting that house in shape. You told me yourself what a mess it is."

"*Jah,* I did, and I will have a time of fixing it, but I know I can find time to write to you every day. But if it will make you feel better, I'll mail the letters once a week all bundled up together." He smiled weakly at her and she found herself wanting to return the smile, even though it was the last thing her lips wanted to do right this minute.

"It won't be forever. Once *Mamm* gets better and the house is live-able for her..." he didn't finish the sentence. They both knew there was a chance his *Mamm* might not get well enough that he could leave her all alone.

He pulled her close again and this time she stopped fighting them and just let the tears fall. He was going and only *Gotte* knew when he would return.

Why, Gotte? Why would you bring me here, let me find him, only to take him away from me? Wasn't it enough that I lost Dat? Wasn't it enough that I grew up lonely... never fitting in with the others?

Could they be right? Is there some wickedness in me that makes it impossible for you to bless my life? Is there something I have done, something that I need to ask forgiveness for? Please forgive me... please...

Please don't take him away from me!

The words poured out of her heart, but she dared not speak them out loud. As desperate as she was for *Gotte* to show her a way out of this mess, she did not want to make this any more difficult for Zeke than it had to be.

At the sound of someone clearing their throat, the two of them pulled apart, but Zeke still didn't let go of her. He glared up at his older *bruder,* who looked at the two of them with an apologetic look on his face, but otherwise showed no sign of moving or going back inside.

"I think that means it's time to go." He let go of her shoulders, but he put one hand on either side of her face and looked deep into her eyes.

"We are not finished. I will be back for you. You just hold on to that."

She couldn't get any words out, but she nodded as he pulled her close again and held her there firmly for a few seconds before letting her go and moving up to the porch.

"I am sorry about this, Rebekah. If there was anything else we could do, you have to know we would." Rebekah wished Zeke's *bruder* sounded less miserable about the whole thing. It would make it much easier for her to be angry with him. But his voice was filled with sadness—and not only for their *mamm's* condition. Of course, she couldn't be angry with him. However, she didn't really trust her voice so she didn't answer, only nodded her head before turning away and moving to the waiting buggy.

Before she took two steps, there was a sound of feet crunching on the snow behind her and then she was being whirled around and lifted off her feet—and, before she could even get her bearings, Zeke was kissing her.

He wrapped his arms around her waist and she wrapped her arms around his neck as he kissed her senseless. When his lips finally left hers, it was only so he could rain kisses all over her face.

As she gasped in surprise, he moved to kiss her tear-soaked cheeks and her forehead and then his lips moved back to hers as she held on to him, wishing this moment would never end.

Even though she knew it would have to end eventually, she was determined to hold on to every second she could get in his arms. She enjoyed his kisses, but what mattered the most was knowing how much he cared for her, and that was what was breaking her heart.

Finally, she had found someone who cared for her, just the way she was, and he was leaving. It might not be forever, but even if it was only for a day, it would be for too long for her taste.

And they both knew it could be years before Reba Hershberger would be able to be on her own again... and that would only be if she managed to heal enough so that she could take care of herself.

Oh, how she wanted to tell him she would go with him. She had wanted to pack her things the minute he told her he was leaving—but *Mamm had...*

"Now you know," Zeke whispered, his forehead leaning up against hers, "You are the *maedel* I intend to marry." And then he kissed her once more before he set her on her feet.

When he walked away, she wanted to call out to him, but she knew it would only make it more difficult for him to go, so she clenched her hands into fists to stop herself. She would not *kumme* between him and his *mamm.*

Icy fingers chased away the warmth that his declaration had filled her with and clenched around her heart as she stood there, watching him walk away from her. Tears poured down her cheeks despite the cold wind that whipped loose tendrils of hair against her face.

Once her vision blurred to the point where she could no longer see Zeke, she raised a hand to impatiently wipe them away, but they continued to fall.

Zeke climbed into the van that had been waiting there for him, and with one more look back at Rebekah, he pulled the side door closed and sat back. A moment later the vehicle began to move down the driveway. She kept her eyes trained on Zeke's face. He was turned to look at her and he had a hand pressed to the window beside him.

Once the van had moved down the driveway and out of sight, Rebekah lost the battle with her shaking legs and dropped to the frozen ground, tears spilling over the hands she raised to cover her face.

She barely noticed the strong arms that lifted her and carried her to the waiting buggy.

.   .   .

Naomi walked out of Rebekah's room and into Samuel's open arms. Resting her head on his chest, she fought the tears she had fought against all evening.

"Why, Samuel?"

"I don't know, *lieb*." He tucked Naomi's head under his chin and held her tightly to him as she let go of a few tears that sneaked past her guard.

"I don't know what to do for her."

"Naomi, I don't think there is anything we can do, except pray. Only *Gotte* knows what his plans are and we cannot hope to understand them."

They stood there for a long time, listening to the broken sobs that could still be heard behind Rebekah and Leah's bedroom door. Rebekah may have finally drifted off to sleep, but her heart-break was still making itself known in the sobs that even sleep could not settle.

"Is Leah..." Samuel asked; moving back enough to look down at Naomi. He wasn't really sure what he wanted to say, but Naomi picked up on his meaning.

"*Jah.* She won't leave Rebekah's side. I tried, but she said she knew just how her *schweschder* feels and she must stay by her—especially now." Swallowing back more tears, Naomi added, "she's such a *gut maedel.*"

Samuel wrapped his arms around Naomi again and they waited together until the door opened and Leah walked out, quietly pulling it closed behind her.

She jumped a little when she saw Naomi and Samuel standing nearby, but then she walked into their embrace and the three of them stood there together for several minutes until Leah gently pulled away.

Naomi figured out right away what had finally forced Leah away from Rebekah's side. She nodded at Leah as she backed away from them and turned to go down the hall.

Samuel turned his head to follow Leah's progress

until he realized where she was headed and then he turned back to Naomi.

"It was so much easier when I could fix it with a hug and a band-aid."

"Something tells me at the time you did not think it was easier," Naomi returned with a hint of a smile, and she felt some of the weight fall off her shoulders when he chuckled in return.

"*Jah,* you are right about that—but it certainly seems easier now when I think on it."

Naomi looked down the hall and then back at the door of the room where her *dochder* slept—alone, with a broken heart. She found that she agreed with Samuel completely; she would do almost anything to be able to erase the hurt for Rebekah. She longed for the days when a hug and a band-aid had been all she needed to make it all better.

. . .

Leah took a moment, her hand on the doorknob of the bathroom. Were they still standing there in the hall? Would they have questions for her; things she wouldn't be able to answer?

To think I introduced the two of them.

The words sounded in her head, but there was no

strength behind them. She could never have known what was going to happen when she had introduced Rebekah to Zeke.

Who could have guessed that the two of them would become attached so quickly?

Certainly not me...

Zeke, who had taken a nearly impossible long time with every decision for as long as she had known him... Rebekah who had been so horrified at the speed *Dat* and Naomi had gotten married...

Who could possibly have guessed that, less than a month after declaring himself, Zeke would be on his way to Pinecraft with his *Mamm,* forced to leave Rebekah behind?

Now Rebekah was stuck here with a broken heart and Leah had no idea what to do for her new *schweschder.* All she could seem to do was sit by Rebekah's bed and pat her hand gently. Leah could not say that she knew exactly how her *schweschder* felt, but she knew how much it hurt to consider losing Jacob in the same way.

At least Rebekah has just turned seventeen. She will only have one more year before she can go after Zeke.

That idea did not seem to make any difference to her, though. Leah had mentioned it and Rebekah had just laid there, crying. *I suppose I would, too. A lot can happen in a year.* She knew that better than anyone, given what had happened within their own family over the past year.

Finally, she made herself open the door. As soon as she stepped into the hall, she could see Naomi standing there, waiting for her. At least *Dat* was nowhere to be found.

"Leah, *danki* for sitting with Rebekah. I confess, I do not know what to do for her. This is so different than what she went through when her *dat* passed away; it is unfamiliar ground for me." Naomi stepped forward to wrap Leah in a warm hug.

Leah returned the hug, wrapping her arms around Naomi's thin frame.

"What will we do, *Mamm?*" Leah didn't see the fresh tears that slid from under Naomi's lashes when she unconsciously used the familiar term.

Leah felt Naomi's arms tighten and snuggled deeper into the comforting warmth she had missed for so many years. She had taken on this responsibility—to sit with her *schweschder* in this first *nacht,* but she saw now that she had support; she had help.

She was not alone anymore.

They stood there for several more moments—Leah gathering strength from Naomi's strong embrace—before they turned and walked down the hall.

Together they would resume the vigil with Rebekah.

NINETEEN

Zeke watched as the landscape changed outside his window, from the farms he knew, to the city, which was unfamiliar to him. It seemed to him that everything was happening in slow motion. He had felt as if he was in a daze since the van had pulled away from Rebekah—and his future with her.

Ha had insisted many times over the last three weeks that he would be back for her; that he would be coming back and they would be married.

But there was a nagging doubt in his mind. It was almost as if a voice was telling him over and over that she would not wait for him... that he would be gone too long... that some other young man in the community would see how special she was and make her his frau.

It had happened with Leah. He had been so certain they had a future. He had waited for years to say something to her and then she had *kumme* into town looking *verhuddelt* and he had been so certain it was the wrong time.

But that voice had nagged at him until he had found himself going to her *haus*. He had wanted to see her, but when her *dat* had answered the door, he had lost his nerve and asked Samuel if he could drive Leah to the gathering that *nacht*.

He could never have guessed that she was already seeing someone else. She had not said a thing to anyone —and why should she, since her young man lived in a different district.

Then, only moments after they arrived, her *freind* had dragged her off and he had not seen her again until his *bruders* had brought the sleigh out. He had thought that an extra ride or two might make her realize how strongly he felt about her, but each time she had jumped out with her *freind* and rushed off. Finally, he had driven her home, yet she'd barely said two words to him.

He had told himself she was not avoiding him in the weeks that followed. She was busy—that was all. Her *bruder* David had been married and then a week later, her *dat* had married Rebekah's *mamm*.

He could still remember the day Rebekah had driven through town with her family. He had just *kumme* out of the general store. He had looked up and seen the most angelic face peering through the small side window of the Fisher's large buggy.

And then, nearly a week later, he had spotted Leah in town and *kumme* over to speak to her, and there she had been—his angel. She had looked down at him from the seat of the buggy and he had looked back up at her, feeling almost as if he had gotten a glimpse of heaven.

That Leah had nearly shoved the two of them together had not sunk into his muddled head until much later—after he had met Jacob and begun to put the whole picture together.

Once he had realized that Leah and Jacob had been seeing each other for at least several weeks, he had figured out that Leah had pushed him toward Rebekah. But it hadn't mattered one bit to him; he had wanted to be with her.

It had *kumme* to him then, that he had only ever felt friendship for Leah—or perhaps a brotherly affection. Indeed, he had not felt any of the emotions he felt for Rebekah, and he had known then that he intended to spend the rest of his life with her.

And he had floated on that knowledge for weeks.

When they attended the community's annual skating party, he had made his intentions obvious to anyone who took notice.

Rebekah had no way of knowing—and perhaps he should have warned her—that the party was where quite a few of the young people made their choices or intentions known, but he had wanted to take no chances of things changing.

So she hadn't really understood. And when they had gone over to her parents and Samuel had congratulated him, he had worried that it had frightened Rebekah. And then he had practically dragged her to the hospital with him. She had kept up a brave front, but what if it had only been that... a front?

What if she was glad to be rid of him? What if she had just been waiting for some excuse to get out of the loose promises they had made to each other?

That's lecherich... She was broken-hearted. She was weeping when you walked away from her.

And she had been; he remembered all too well the feel of her tears against his cheeks as he swooped in and kissed her.

She kissed you back.

He could remember how her arms had clung to him; as if she never wanted to let go. She had held tightly to him as their lips had met and he had felt the urgency in her grip.

I did not imagine that.

No, he couldn't have. But he had no other experience with kissing to compare it to. Could he have thought it was wonderful, but it didn't mean the same to her?

I need to stop this, he told himself. No good would *kumme* of second-guessing himself. The fact remained that he was on his way to Florida and she was in New York; and for the time being, that was how it would remain.

.   .   .

"Zeke, you have to wake up." Someone was shaking him, but his sleep-fogged brain had no idea who.

"*Kumme* on, Zeke. The train is going to leave. We don't have much time." Finally, Zeke recognized his *bruder's* voice and he sat up, trying to clear the fog so he could think straight.

Where am I?

And it all came crashing back to him. *Mamm's accident... Florida... leaving Rebekah.* With each thought came a new wave of hurt and with the last, he was surprised to feel anger blossom within him. He pushed it down as he stumbled out of the van.

"I cannot believe you fell asleep." Thomas was saying as he loaded luggage and boxes onto a long rolling cart. Zeke turned to help his *bruder,* still trying to shake off sleep.

He couldn't believe he had fallen asleep, either. Of course he had been up most of the last three *nachts* packing his things and *Mamm's.* Worrying that *Mamm* might not get better, although the doctor had said otherwise. Worrying about the transition to Florida. Worrying about leaving Rebekah. Exhaustion must have finally caught up to him on the drive to the train depot.

When the last piece of luggage was loaded, Thomas clapped a hand on Zeke's shoulder and squeezed. Zeke knew it was Thomas' way of showing his support in a way he would never be able to voice.

Thomas was the most compassionate of them, but he was also the one who had the most trouble with expressing his emotions. Zeke had a moment to think of what a tough time his new *frau* must have had with knowing how Thomas felt about her. But he knew there were other ways to speak your emotions and he was certain Thomas and Cora communicated their feelings just fine.

Thomas nodded his head at Zeke and began pushing the loaded-down cart toward the train station. Zeke looked at it and knew that it did not contain everything they had packed into the back of the van. Thomas must have let him sleep while he loaded up at least one load of cargo to check onto the train.

"Zeke," He turned at the sound of his name and the driver was standing there with a hand out. Zeke put his hand into Phil's, and the man pulled him into a quick hug. Only a second later, he released Zeke and finished his sentence, still firmly shaking Zeke's hand.

"You'll be missed around here, boy. You take care down there, hear?"

Zeke nodded, surprised to find that his throat felt like it was closing up. The unexpected emotion choked him a little as the man he had known most of his life finally let go of his hand and gave him a hard clout on the back before turning back to the waiting van and climbing into the driver's seat.

"You tell Thomas I'll be right here when he's ready to head back. And tell your ma I'll be praying for her."

"*Danki* Phil, I certainly will. That means a lot." Zeke managed to get the few words out before his voice started to crack. He turned, embarrassed now to be showing such emotion so publicly.

He could just see Thomas, as his tall, thin *bruder* made his way through the crowd, pushing the loaded cart. He picked up the two cases he would be taking with him and headed for the main part of the station.

Halfway across the crowded lot, he saw *Mamm's* doctor. He was looking through the crowd, probably searching for either him or Thomas, so Zeke made his way to the man. When Dr. Zimmerman saw him, he seemed to relax a little and stepped forward to meet Zeke halfway.

"She's fine, Zeke. She's all settled. You remember me telling you about the young lady who was working with me here?" At Zeke's nod, he went on. "She's with your mother and she plans to stay with her the entire trip. You may want to spell her now and then so she can have a bit of a stretch, but the compartment has facilities, and I've arranged for meals to be brought to them unless Marie tells them otherwise."

"Now don't forget that you're changing trains in about nine hours. I've already spoken to a good friend there and he has agreed to help Marie get your mother from one train to the other, so you don't have anything to worry about." He laughed as he said it and then at Zeke's bewildered expression, he explained.

"John is a bit of a character. When I told him about it, he was very excited to meet you all." He laughed again before saying, "Just don't be surprised if he makes a big fuss over you. Though I expect your mother won't mind one bit as long as it makes her transition as painless as possible."

After a moment, he added, "And the special transport van is going to meet you at the station in Orlando." He clapped a hand on Zeke's shoulder then.

"It's a good thing you're doing, son. Not many young men these days would give up their home, their family, their community and..." he cleared his throat, but stopped a moment, before he went on, but something in his tone made Zeke wonder if he knew a bit more about who Zeke was leaving behind.

"Between the warmth and the physical therapy I've set up down there, your mother should make a full recovery within the year." After a moment he added, "Now you understand, even after a full recovery, she may not want to move north again. Bones may heal, but she'll always feel the cold in them and it will make her arthritis worse, so she may decide she wants to stay down there even after she's recovered."

"Of course, once she's all better, she should be able to take care of herself so..." he trailed off again and Zeke felt certain the doctor knew about Rebekah. He felt some better knowing the man was trying to encourage him, but they had a long road ahead of them and he didn't want to put the cart before the horse.

"We appreciate everything you've done for us, doctor." and Zeke set down one of his cases to shake the man's hand.

"Just doing my job, son."

"*Nee,* I don't think that's true. You have done so much for us. None of us would have known where to start or what would have been needed to help *Mamm.* Not only did you spend extra time giving us instruction, you've made arrangements for special care and travel. Our family owes you much and we are grateful."

He didn't say what came to mind, but he could not help but think that, without Dr. Zimmerman, they wouldn't have *Mamm* right now. *Gotte* had clearly sent him to them in their time of need, and as he stood there looking at the doctor, Zeke realized his thoughts were reflected in the man's eyes.

He nodded and Zeke thought it must be his way of saying that he knew what else Zeke wanted to say. He began to let go of the doctor's hand, but the man pulled him into a hug much like the one he had just received from Phil.

Zeke didn't know what to think of all the emotion he was suddenly on the receiving end of. Either he was going to be missed a lot more than he had realized or everyone knew about Rebekah already and they were sympathetic.

Could it be that they know what I have only guessed at—that she will not wait for me, and some other young man will claim her before I can return? He shut those thoughts out of his head. Even if it were true, it would not do to dwell on such things.

Gotte had them all in his hand and he would guide their paths. And if Rebekah was not the *maedel Gotte* intended for Zeke, it would be best to turn his mind to other things.

Finally the doctor released his hand and nodded again.

"Godspeed, young man." He slipped a small paper into Zeke's hand as he stepped back. "The doctor in Florida has all my information, but I want you to have this, just in case. You can call me anytime. If I don't answer, just leave me a message with a number where I can reach you. I'll get back to you as quickly as I can." And then he turned and walked past Zeke, heading for the exit. Zeke slipped the paper into his pocket and picked up his cases.

He had lost sight of Thomas, but he thought he remembered where he was supposed to go. *Mamm* would be in a special room for the trip but he had a regular seat in the car behind hers. The doctor had made a point of telling him that he would be close to *Mamm.* Zeke thought again of how much the doctor had done for their family. He was a *gut* man indeed.

He wound his way through the crowded station,

following the signs that led him to the trains. He had to ask twice about which platform he was supposed to head for, but he finally found the right one, thanking *Gotte* for the kindness of the workers here.

When he finally reached the train, he looked around for Thomas, but his *bruder* was nowhere to be found. Zeke had just decided to look for Thomas on board when he saw his *bruder's* tall form as he stepped down from the last car.

Thomas raised a hand to wave and headed right for him. Zeke started in the direction his *bruder* was coming, thinking maybe that was the car he was supposed to be on, but halfway there, Thomas waved a hand at Zeke and motioned for him to stop.

His *bruder* was saying something, but Zeke couldn't hear him. Then he realized that Thomas was waving at the car that was right next to Zeke. He looked over at it and surely enough, it was the number he was looking for.

He stopped by the door and then moved a few steps forward to make way for passengers that were slipping by him onto the train. No one stopped to say anything to him, they just quickly moved past him and stepped on board. Zeke was happy to have even a small break from the unexpected onslaught of emotions from people telling him goodbye.

Thomas continued to walk toward him, weaving his way through the crowd that was quickly thinning out. Zeke looked at the large clock that was suspended from the station ceiling a few feet from him. He had a few more minutes before the train left. Thomas wouldn't have long to relay his own goodbye, but Zeke didn't see it taking more than a minute or two anyway.

"*Mamm's* all settled. That nice *maedel* from Dr. Zimmerman's office is with her. It was a *gut* thing she happened to be heading down that way to visit her family." Thomas took one of Zeke's cases from him and stepped on board the train.

Zeke followed his *bruder,* surprised that Thomas felt the need to settle him on the train. When he stepped on board, he was surprised to see that the car Thomas had stepped onto held no seats, but had a long hallway where there must be private compartments.

"Thomas, this cannot be the right car. I'm meant to have a seat, not a compartment." he looked down at his ticket and he could see it said a number, but there was nothing about it that told whether he was looking for a seat or a compartment.

"I know you said you didn't want to cost anyone more money, but it's a long way to Florida, *bruder.*" He took hold of Zeke's shoulder again and squeezed. "And you'll be sitting up long enough in the van that will take you the rest of the way from the train station in Orlando.

Zeke didn't know what to think when he looked at his *bruder*. Thomas had never been one to express emotion easily, but there were strong emotions in his eyes as he gripped Zeke's shoulder.

"We were not about to let you sit up all that way." He turned and led Zeke into a small compartment. "*Mamm's* compartment is at the other end of this car, since it has to have extra room for the hospital bed and space for her companion to move around her, but you're still close."

"I've been in to see her and she's all settled. She made me promise to *kumme* down to visit as soon as I'm able. Since we've already paid for the tickets to visit Seth and Stephen and their families in Ohio, Cora and I simply cannot afford to not go. But as soon as we're back, we will settle things here and head down to Florida to spare you."

"Do not rush on my account, Thomas. *Mamm* and I will be fine." After a moment, he added, "And don't forget how much work I'm going to have, getting that *haus* in shape. It will be quite a while before I'm finished with even the most basic repairs."

Thomas laughed then. "At least you'll be able to do the repairs without freezing your fingers off."

And Zeke was surprised to find himself laughing with his *bruder*. The weather would be considerably warmer in Florida. That was the only *gut* thing he could think of about this trip.

He prayed the doctor was right, and that the weather would help *Mamm* get better... real soon.

TWENTY

Rebekah looked up from the dough she was kneading when she heard Jacob's voice, followed a moment later by Leah's laughter. Quickly she looked around, wishing there was some way for her to escape. The last thing she wanted to hear right now was the happy couple.

However, her hands and wrists were covered in flour and sticky dough, so she would most likely be stuck here—at least until she finished and the bread was safely in the pans. She tried to knead faster, but the dough was not cooperating, so instead she stopped and said a prayer.

Please Gotte, help me to be charitable? Please take

this pain away from me. Heal my heart Lord, please?

"Rebekah, I didn't know you were here." The pity in her cousin's voice was almost more than she could take, but she made the effort to smile so he would hear it in her voice as she answered.

"*Jah,* just making bread." and she waved one doughy hand in the air so he would not wonder why she didn't turn.

"Do you need help?" This came from Leah and Rebekah was at least comforted when she heard no pity in her new *schweschder's* voice.

"*Nee,* I am already up to my elbows in the dough." She tried to add a little laugh at the end, but even she could hear the false sound to it.

There was no noise behind her as she continued to knead and work the dough. Clearly Leah was unsure of whether to not to leave Rebekah alone and Jacob was certainly not going to go off and leave Leah alone.

They were all saved by Lillian's entrance. She bounced into the room and, in the way of a bubbly *kind,* sensed none of the tension in the air. She walked right over to Rebekah and raised up on her toes beside her new *schweschder.*

"Ooh, can I help?" Her voice was so hopeful, so full of longing, and with no trace of pity, that Rebekah felt a genuine smile make it's way onto her features.

Immediately she felt better and she turned to Leah.

"Looks like I have all the help I need. *Danki.*" She was relieved to see Leah smile back at her before turning to Jacob.

"*Kumme* on, Jacob. You know what they say about too many cooks in the kitchen." The last thing Rebekah saw before turning back was Leah pulling Jacob by his sleeve.

She was surprised to feel laughter, real laughter bubbling up inside her. She knew it had been the image of her tall, strong, cousin being pulled out of the room by a tiny *maedel* that was tickling her, but it felt so *gut* to laugh again.

Rebekah turned back to the counter and saw that Lillian was pulling a step stool over to the counter. She looked over at the smile on her new little *schweschder's* face and could not help but smile in return.

It was *gut* to have a younger *schweschder*. Rebekah had not anticipated how much she would enjoy spending time with Lillian. *And now that I no longer have a young man...* the thought trailed off as a sharp pain speared through her heart.

"Rebekah, *was iss letz?*" Lillian asked and Rebekah turned away from the young *maedel*, trying desperately to get herself under control.

"Are you sad about Zeke going away?" The question

surprised Rebekah enough to distract her from the pain in her heart. How did Lillian even know about Zeke? Rebekah looked back at Lillian and was surprised to see a knowing smile on her young face.

"I heard *Mamm* and Leah talking about it," she said, in the way of a young *maedel* who has not a worry in the world.

"They said all you need is time." She looked up at Rebekah then. "I don't understand though. How will time heal your heart? Time just passes; it doesn't really do anything, does it?" She just stood there, looking up at Rebekah, while she waited for the answer.

"Well, the time doesn't really do anything." Rebekah stopped a moment to think before she went on. She did not want to tell Lillian the wrong thing. She also did not want to frighten the young *maedel.* "I think what they mean is, as time passes, my heart will hurt less."

"Oh! Well, that makes a lot more sense." Lillian smiled and moved over to the cabinet. A moment later, she returned with the loaf pans, setting them on the countertop nearest them.

Rebekah watched her, as she moved around the kitchen picking up things Rebekah would need for the bread. She thought about the sweet smile on Lillian's face; about the way Lillian had accepted her answer so quickly... so easily.

There was such trust in her new *schweschder;* even though Rebekah did not feel like she had really done anything to earn that trust, Lillian had given it.

Rebekah felt the smile return to her face. She felt warmth creep into her for the first time in days. It was a *gut* feeling.

.   .   .

"I am worried for Rebekah." Jacob said to Leah as they walked out onto the back porch.

"*Jah,* I am as well... but I have no idea what to do for her." Leah looked up at Jacob as she spoke. He was so tall and strong, just being with him made her feel safe and cared for. What would she do if ever she lost him?

At the thought, an shudder rippled through her and with it came a deeper understanding of what Rebekah must be feeling. It made Leah think of how she felt when she had lost *Mamm.* The world had suddenly felt dark and cold and small, and she had felt lost and all alone.

"She has already been through so much in her life." Jacob's words interrupted her thoughts and she looked up at him and nodded.

"But then, so have you," he added, almost as if he had just remembered that Leah had lost her own *Mamm* at a young age.

Not that she could blame him for not remembering, given that he was from a different district... not to mention how seamlessly Naomi had fitted into their family. They were like a whole new family now. Even Rebekah had found her place in the family; it was the one consolation Leah could think of. Rebekah had lost Zeke, but she had all of them to help her get through it all.

It still sounded like too little to Leah, but she had to trust that *Gotte* knew what he was doing with the situation. He must...

If anyone knew what was best for everyone involved, it would certainly be *Gotte*.

TWENTY-ONE

Zeke stood on the cracked sidewalk that led to the sagging porch. He had prayed all the way across it earlier today, as he had helped the young nurse who Dr. Zimmerman had sent with them to wheel *Mamm's* support chair into the *haus*.

The nurse had quickly and quietly made up the bed with clean sheets and gotten *Mamm* tucked safely beneath them with no help at all. Then she went about putting the room in order. He was grateful to have her there to help with *Mamm*.

Although Simon had made arrangements for the house to be cleaned before Zeke and his *mamm* arrived, there was still much to be done to make it habitable—

and safe. Most of the repairs he could handle, but tending to *Mamm* and her extensive injuries was not something he was prepared for.

Thankfully, the doctor had made arrangements with one of his nurses, who would be dividing her time between caring for his *mamm* and visiting her own family who lived nearby.

As soon as *Mamm* was settled, and resting peacefully, Zeke had made his way through each room, adding items to his ever-growing list of things to do.

Mamm's room was in the best shape. A fresh coat of paint on the ceiling and walls would be the only improvement needed, but Zeke wouldn't do any painting in the *haus* until *Mamm* was able to spend time outdoors so the paint fumes wouldn't affect her.

The kitchen and bathroom both needed considerable repairs. Replacing the fixtures would be the most expensive improvement in the bathroom, along with new linoleum on the floor. There were also missing tiles in the shower. Zeke suspected he would find wet wall board around the tub; the remaining tiles and sheetrock needed to be replaced as soon as he could get to it.

The *haus* had been rented out for awhile and when the tenants moved out they had left a dirty *haus* and lots of trash. They had never asked for any repairs, but looking around, Zeke wondered in amazement why they had chosen not to... by the look of things, the appliances had not been cleaned in years and there were several broken shelves in the refrigerator. Obviously, the tenants had not been the type of people they should have rented their *haus* to. Zeke even found a couple of walls with fist-sized holes.

It became clear right away that he would need to make a trip into town while the nurse was available to sit with *Mamm*. He would need to buy supplies and start on repairs right away.

. . .

After visiting several local stores, arms laden down with bags, Zeke swiped a hand over his forehead as he walked along the street heading back to their little *haus*. No one else around him seemed to be sweating; they were clearly accustomed to the heat. So far, his body had not been able to adjust to the weather here— and it was only going to get hotter.

He longed for snow... for the thick, evergreen tree outside his window at home, for the way the winter sunlight filtered through it's branches and painted intricate patterns on the floor of his room. He longed for a tall, heavy mug of hot chocolate and the thick, frozen pond, and for skating along it with Rebekah's arm wrapped around his.

He stopped himself and shook his head, trying to clear the thoughts from it. It would do him no *gut* to dwell on these longings when there was nothing he could do to make his wants a reality.

I must learn to be content where I am. Gotte would not want me to forget that I have responsibilities here. And Rebekah would not want me to mope. Thoughts of Rebekah lent speed to his feet. The mail usually came about this time of day. Would there be another letter from her waiting in the small box? Would she have gotten his last one already or would it take several days to reach her?

He really should write again. He had tried to write every day, but caring for *Mamm* and his rush to get the *haus* in *gut* shape wore him out so that he barely made it to his bed some *nachts*.

He was so intent on getting to the mailbox, that he did not immediately notice the man standing on the unfinished porch—a hand raised as if to knock at the door. When his foot landed heavily on the bottom step, the only one he had not had to replace, the man spun around, his hand still in midair and a look of surprise on his face.

When Zeke looked up and saw the man's face, a

strange feeling stirred his thoughts. Something about him was familiar... but Zeke couldn't immediately remember where he knew the man from.

He had exactly three seconds to wonder about it before the man thundered across the porch and threw his arms around Zeke.

"Zeke! Man! Is it good to see you!"

Zeke stood there with his arms full of bags as thoughts raced through his mind. The familiar face... the familiar voice... the familiarity of the greeting...

Could this be...? Is it even possible?

He shook his head again as he tried to make sense of this strange situation. *It couldn't be Tobias... could it?*

After several more seconds, the strong arms finally loosened their hold and Zeke carefully watched the man's face as he stepped back, looking for—and seeing —the resemblance to the young man he remembered. He had not seen Tobias in more than five years.

The first thing he noticed was the way the man in front of him was dressed. He was wearing very much the same thing Zeke had on, except for a few small differences. The sleeves of his shirt were short, only covering a small part of his upper arm. He wore a straw hat, not a black felt one, and the materials his clothing was made of looked different as well—it was much thinner.

Well, that makes sense, I suppose. Who wants to wear such thick, heavy clothing in this heat. Why had it not occurred to Zeke to find some clothing made for the weather here, instead of wearing the clothes he had brought with him—clothes that were made to withstand the harsh northern winter weather?

After nearly a minute, the man shuffled his feet and the look that crossed his face then brought a memory rushing into Zeke's thoughts. He remembered the day his *bruder* had announced he was leaving the community. Zeke had just *kumme* in from his morning chores and he had walked into the kitchen to find *Mamm* and Tobias arguing. Well, Tobias had been arguing. *Mamm* had stood there with her hands tucked under her apron.

Neither of them had seen Zeke as he stood there as quietly as possible, while he tried to decide what he should do. He didn't know whether it would be better to turn and go back the way he had *kumme* or make some noise to announce his presence.

After several seconds, Tobias had finally stopped arguing and hung his head, and when he'd looked back up at *Mamm,* he had looked just like the man in front of Zeke looked now.

He must have made some noise, or recognition

must have flickered across his own face because Tobias stepped forward then and held out a hand to Zeke.

"I know it's been a long time, but do you think you could find it in your heart to forgive me?" Zeke felt the bags slide from his fingers as he stepped forward to embrace his *bruder*.

When they stepped back again, Zeke was surprised to see tears glistening in his *bruder's* eyes. Tobias covered them well by laughing and swiping a hand half-heartedly at Zeke.

"Little *bruder*, I do believe you've grown a foot since I last saw you."

Zeke laughed in return. "I'm not so little anymore, Tobias."

Thoughts of all Tobias had missed in the years since he had left them crowded into Zeke's memory then and he looked back at his *bruder*. There were so many questions bouncing around his head, he didn't know where to begin.

Tobias looked as if he was trying to read Zeke's thoughts. He nodded and then after a moment he spoke, a serious expression taking over his features. "I know. You have a million questions and I'm certain the first one is where I've been all this time. Or perhaps why I am dressed plain... since I left the community."

Zeke nodded as he answered. "*Jah,* a million

questions."

"First, let's start with getting these groceries and supplies in the house, yeah?"

Zeke had a moment to think that Tobias sounded more like an *Englischer* now, as they gathered up the bags Zeke had dropped in his hurry to embrace his long-lost *bruder.* Then, as the two of them carried the bags inside, more questions came to him.

Undoubtedly, Tobias would tell him where he had been all this time, as well as why he was dressed plain—especially since he had brought both things up. But Zeke could not help but wonder about why Tobias was not also speaking plain, and why he had not told anyone in the family anything about where he had been and what he had been doing since he left home.

Or maybe he did. Maybe he spoke to Thomas or Timothy or Simon and they told him how he could find us. Nothing else made sense as far as how he knew to find them here—at the *haus* in Pinecraft.

Once the groceries and medication Zeke had picked up had been put away, he turned to look at Tobias. His *bruder* had certainly grown up in the last five years. He only loosely resembled the young man he had been back then, though he did look more like their eldest *bruder* Simon than he had before.

Which is likely the only reason I recognized him.

"I guess you're wondering how I knew where to find you..."

"*Jah,* that is one of the things I am wondering.*"

"Well, actually, that is the easiest thing to explain." When Zeke said nothing, he went on. "I wrote home a few months ago."

Zeke waited, and after a minute, Tobias kept going. "Mom and I have been talking on the phone once a week since then." Before Zeke could ask, he added, "I call on the barn phone at the same time each week. Mom makes sure she's there to answer. But when I called last night, Simon answered."

"*Jah,* he was waiting for a call from me."

"Yeah, that's what he said."

"And he told you what had happened to *Mamm?*"

"Not at first, no. We talked for a long time before he told me about the accident. And it was even longer before he told me you were down here with her, fixing up the old place and taking care of her. Speaking of which, who is with her now?"

"A nurse who has family nearby. The doctor from Clearview made arrangements for her to travel with us. She sits with *Mamm* each day so that I can work on the *haus* or go into the village if I need to."

"How is she?" For the first time since Zeke had seen him, Tobias sounded like he had when he had argued with *Mamm* in the kitchen five years ago—more like a young boy than a man.

Zeke answered as honestly as he could, trying at the same time to inject more hope into the words than he felt. "The doctor says that she has a *gut* chance of a full recovery, especially here in this warm climate."

"Yeah, Windy Gap would not be the place for an easy recovery of any sort."

They both laughed at that before Zeke went on with his explanation. "It's only been a few days here, but I feel like she is already resting easier and she looks as if she is in less pain than she was before we left."

"That sounds good... hopeful."

"*Jah.*"

"So, what can I do? How can I help? Would it be better if I sat with Mom while you fix up the house, or if I work on the house while you sit with her?"

Zeke had to laugh at that. His *bruder* had been the least skilled of them all at making home repairs, though he had certainly had a way with wood and metal work. "I think, of the two choices given, I would prefer you help with *Mamm* and leave the repairs to me."

"You can laugh, but I have learned a lot in the last five years. You would be surprised at what I've been doing."

"*Jah? Like what?*"

"Yeah. Well, I've learned quite a lot. I've worked with several different contractors over the last few years. I've learned everything about building a house, new from the ground up, or repairing an older one." He spoke so assuredly about it, Zeke couldn't find a way to argue.

In fact, when he looked at his *bruder,* he could see just how serious he was about the whole thing.

But why would he do that? He was never interested in building before.

Tobias must have seen something in Zeke's expression to give away what he was thinking. "I know what you're thinking. I was never interested in home repairs when I was growing up."

Zeke nodded, and Tobias continued. "It was the only job that I could find, with an eighth grade education and no other experience." He stopped for a moment. "Even all of my skill with metal-working was useless." He waved a hand dismissively, then. "Oh, it came in handy later, but at first, to get a job, it was pretty much worthless."

Zeke waited for his *bruder* to continue, but Tobias remained quiet. Finally Zeke spoke.

"So, you took a job with a contractor... why? And what happened then?" He wanted answers and Tobias had said he would give them.

"Well, I traveled for a while with this one company. That company changed hands a couple of times. Then I ended up with another company, a much smaller one."

Zeke nodded, thinking to himself that Tobias was leaving out big pieces of information that he would likely have to press for later on.

"One of their jobs was here in Pinecraft. We worked here for over a year, and when the company finished the job, they moved on." He shrugged. "I decided to stay."

It was pretty obvious there was more to the story, but again, Zeke left it alone, hoping that he would have the time later to get the whole story.

"Well, *bruder*. You've come a long ways to see *mamm*. Let's go see if she's awake and ready for a visit."

Leading the way, Zeke moved toward his *mamm's* room, his *bruder* following close behind him.

TWENTY-TWO

Zeke watched the reunion between his *mamm* and his *bruder. He* was forced to admit that having her son there with her, especially after all this time away, looked to be doing some *gut* for her health.

She was smiling and talking, and more animated than he had seen her in days. *Jah,* it could be the warmth, but he chose to believe that it was the relief of a mother who had been missing her son for five years.

It looked to be doing some *gut* for Tobias, as well. His smile was wider, his tone of voice—which had been full of nerves—was relaxed now, and some of the tension had left his shoulders.

He looked more like the *bruder* that Zeke

remembered from more than five years ago. It was almost as if no time had passed, as if he had never left, but as if he had simply *kumme* to Florida to work, like their eldest *bruders* had moved to Ohio. And Zeke found himself wishing it was true, that the last five years had been different, and that Tobias had never left them the way he had.

It was so *gut* to have the family back together this way. Even though they were not all together, it felt as if they were. Tobias being here was nearly enough to make Zeke forget how miserable he had been for the last week.

Almost...

After several minutes of watching from the doorway, Zeke decided he would go and get some work done on the *haus* while Tobias and *Mamm* caught up on the last five years.

There will be plenty of time for me to catch up with him later. So long as Tobias did not leave them the same way again, he would have all the time in the world to hear about the last five years of his *bruder's* life.

. . .

Nearly a week passed, with the two *bruders*

following the same course. Every day, Zeke would work on repairs while the nurse kept *Mamm* company. He tackled the worst of the repairs first, determined to get the *haus* back into the shape it was before the previous tenants had wrecked it. The doctor had told him there was very little chance *Mamm* would ever be able to make it through a New York winter again, so the little *haus* in Pinecraft would be hers from then on.

He only took time out from the repairs to build a ramp at one end of the front porch. He knew *Mamm* too well to think that she would be content to stay in the *haus* all the time. She would want to venture out as soon as she was able; having the ramp already in place would give her no room to argue about going out in the special support chair that was designed to take the worst of the pressure off her injuries.

Each day Tobias arrived about an hour after the nurse left, giving Zeke time alone with *Mamm*. Then, when he arrived, they would have an early supper together, talking over things they had missed out on the last five years.

. . .

Tobias had already told Zeke about some of his work, but he told *Mamm* even more during their long talks. He had moved around a lot as jobs ended, constantly in search of something that he did not know how to explain.

During his travels, he had spoken and dressed like the *Englishers* around him, only talking about his plain lifestyle when absolutely necessary.

Zeke was certain he was not the only one who noticed the pain that flickered in *Mamm's* eyes, but when he moved to get up, she waved him away, and told Tobias to go on.

The more Tobias told them about his time away from the family, the more Zeke found himself wondering what it was that had kept Tobias from coming back to them. Nothing in his explanations sounded like a *gut* enough reason to stay away.

.   .   .

And then, just one week after arriving in Pinecraft, Zeke was busy securing loose shingles when he noticed Tobias heading up the front walkway with a young woman he did not recognize.

Before they could disappear beneath the roof over the porch, Zeke called out. Tobias looked up with a smile and waved his *bruder* down. "Zeke, come meet Lydia."

Zeke was quick to set aside his tools and climb down from the roof, thinking the whole way down how much he had obviously missed. He wanted to be angry with Tobias, but at the same time, he could only be grateful to see his *bruder* again.

His feet had no more than hit the ground than Tobias was introducing the young *maedel* with him. "Zeke, this is Lydia Troyer." His voice was filled with more excitement than Zeke could remember ever hearing. "And Lydia, this is my baby brother, Zeke."

Zeke quickly covered his surprised laugh with a cough. Baby *bruder*. . . really? It has been a long time.

"He does not look like much of a baby to me." When Lydia spoke, her voice was very quiet, not at all what he had been expecting.

He also did not expect the expression on his *bruder's* face. His expression made it clear that Lydia was the most important person in all the world. Why, my *bruder* has gone and grown up.

"Well, should we go in and meet your *mamm*, Tobias?" Lydia spoke after several long, silent moments. Zeke watched as Tobias nearly tripped over his own feet, turning toward the front porch again.

Zeke trailed along behind the couple, watching them as they moved across the porch and into the small *haus*. Tobias pulled open the screened door, then pushed the front door open, then waited for Lydia to move through the doorway before following her. It was odd to see his wild *bruder* so calm and obviously taken with the young *maedel*. Zeke was more than a little surprised that his *bruder* had never mentioned her during their time together.

When they walked into *Mamm's* room, it was clear that was not the case. She might never have met Lydia, but clearly Tobias had already told *Mamm* all about her.

She greeted the young woman like a *freind*, her face lighting up with excitement.

"So this is the young *maedel* I have heard so much about. *Kumme,* sit. Let us get to know each other." She motioned them forward. Lydia took the narrow seat next to the special bed where *Mamm* rested.

Zeke mostly stayed where he was, leaning against the door frame, while Tobias and Lydia talked with *Mamm* about many things.

He learned that Tobias had *kumme* to Florida to build houses for the *Englischers*. He had been working in Sarasota, but had met Lydia at one of the local restaurants that served plain cooking. Evidently, he had missed plain food.

When his company had moved on, he had not went with them, but had stayed behind and looked for work. He had found a local metal craftsman who had hired him. He made metal sculptures for several of the stores in the area who specialized in Amish-made items. Evidently, they were popular enough with the tourists that Tobias had already bought a small *haus* nearby and begun making a place for himself and Lydia.

Zeke was not surprised when they mentioned their upcoming wedding, but it was a bit of a shock to discover that *Mamm* already seemed to know all about it.

Before he could ask how she knew, they were deep in conversation about plans that had been made.

"I have already spoken with your doctor and he is confident that you will be well enough in time that we won't have to postpone anything."

"Now, Tobias," Lydia spoke quietly. "Let's don't rush your *Mamm*. She needs time to heal, and we are going to make certain she gets it. If we have to put the wedding off, that is what we will do."

Tobias only nodded.

"Nonsense." was *Mamm's* reply. "I will be plenty well enough in a month's time. And if I am not, there's no need to be putting off the wedding on my account. That's just silly."

Lydia did not argue. She just leaned in to take *Mamm's* hand gently in her own. "Then I suppose we will just have to pray very hard and do everything we can to be certain you are plenty healed in time."

Tobias nodded again, his face filled with a smile.

Zeke only stood there, watching the two of them together. And seeing the way his bruder obviously cared for Lydia made him miss Rebekah so much, it hurt to breathe for a moment.

EPILOGUE

Rebekah shuffled through the stack of mail she had just pulled from the box at the end of their gravel lane, her eyes searching for a familiar handwriting.

Zeke had been true to his promise, writing her a letter or sending a postcard every single day since his departure. She was especially fond of the postcard he had sent from the train station in New York City. In one of the busiest cities in the world, he had managed to find a picture of Central Park that was peaceful and calm. It had brought an unexpected warmth to read that he was already missing her sweet smile.

She had tucked the card into her Bible, marking the

passage where Rebekah and her damsels had ridden camels, following the man who would deliver her to her future husband.

The next postcard had been from Orlando, Florida and had shown a silly picture of a cartoon mouse wearing pants. Zeke's note had read, *"These Englischers sure have some strange ideas, jah?"*

She had tucked that one away as well, along with each letter that had arrived since, praying over each one that *Gotte* would watch over Zeke and that his *mamm's* injuries would heal quickly so that they could return to Windy Gap.

For several days after their departure, she had felt that perhaps she was being punished for giving her own *Mamm* such a hard time over getting married... or maybe because she had felt uncharitable toward *Mamm* for a long time after *Dat's* passing. It had been difficult to honor her *Mamm* as the scripture commanded, having spent so much more time with her grandparents as she grew older—and *Dat's* illness had required so much more care.

When *Mamm* had written to her that she would need to *kumme* out to Windy Gap, Rebekah had been very angry, not at all like an obedient *dochder*. She had felt as if *Mamm* had stolen her from the only life she had ever known.

To have found a reason to feel as if she might finally be happy living in Windy Gap—only to have it snatched away—felt like the worst punishment she could imagine. And more than a few pages of her Bible had been stained with tears as she searched for answers and prayed seeking *Gotte's* forgiveness.

Only the postcards and letters gave her hope that Zeke was not lost to her forever—though in some of her darker moments she secretly feared that his *mamm* would never return north... that he would be forced to stay in Florida with her... and that he would meet a nice, young *maedel* there to marry.

She never spoke of her fears to anyone but *Gotte*. However, they plagued her for the few minutes now as she felt of the thickness of the envelope with her name on it.

So soon? How could it be? He has not even been gone two weeks. She placed the rest of the mail on the small table just inside the mudroom door and slipped out of her boots, stealing upstairs as quietly as possible so that she could read the letter in private.

· · ·

Naomi had just walked into the kitchen to begin supper preparations when Rebekah came flying down the stairs, nearly knocking her over in her rush.

She caught hold of her *dochder,* fearing the worst. What if she had received terrible news from her young man in Florida? How would she deal with losing him on top of everything else?

"What is it, Rebekah?"

Rebekah did not answer immediately. She took several deep breaths first, and Naomi braced herself.

"He wants me to *kumme, Mamm.* He wants me to *kumme* to Pinecraft.*"

Naomi started to speak, to interrupt her *dochder,* but Rebekah went on quickly. "He sent me a ticket. The train leaves on the fifteenth of next month. He says that gives his *mamm* plenty of time to recover so she can be there, too."

Rebekah's words worried Naomi. Was Zeke already asking her *dochder* to marry him... in Pinecraft... in only a month!

What would she do? What could she do?

"He says you and *Dat* and the whole family are invited, too. You don't have to *kumme,* but he really wants me to. Is it all right, *Mamm?* Can I go?"

Now Naomi was really confused. For sure Zeke would not be so casual about whether or not Rebekah's parents attended her own wedding. "Rebekah, I think you had better start at the beginning."

Rebekah took another deep breath, and then started again. "Zeke wants me to *kumme* to Pinecraft next month for his *bruder's* wedding."Naomi sighed in relief then, but Rebekah did not even seem to notice, rushing on in her explanation. "They have been planning it for some time now and he says his *mamm* is doing so much better already, the doctor thinks she will be plenty healed enough by next month. And he sent a train ticket for me because he wants me to *kumme*. Is it all right if I go, *Mamm? P*lease?"

She smiled at the hopeful expression on her *dochder's* sweet face. It was the happiest she had seen her in weeks. "I think that would be just fine, Rebekah." The words had no more left her mouth than she had a *wunderbaar* idea. "Why don't you take Leah and your cousin with you, as well. It could be fun for the three of you to go together." *And you would be much safer traveling in a group.* She kept that thought to herself, but smiled when Rebekah's face fairly lit up at her suggestion.

Rebekah threw her arms around Naomi and squeezed tightly. "That is a perfect idea, *Mamm.* I am going to go and tell her now. Then she can ask Jacob tonight about it." And before Naomi could say a word, Rebekah was headed for the mudroom, hurriedly pulling on her boots and then flying out the side door of the *haus*.

"What was all of that about, *lieb?*" Samuel's voice behind her had Naomi smiling for a completely different reason.

"That was our *dochder,* very excited about going to see the young man she has been missing these past few weeks."

Naomi smiled again as Samuel wrapped his arms around her, his voice much closer now. "I knew *Gotte* would find a way to work it all out."

A moment later, his hands stilled, feeling a familiar bump. Samuel kissed her cheek, then turned slightly to whisper into her ear. "Is there something you're waiting to tell me, *mei frau?*"

Naomi giggled. "*Jah.* I have some *wunderbaar* news of my own to share... but only with you—at least for now."

DISCUSSION QUESTIONS
WARNING - SPOILERS AHEAD

1) Rebekah has a difficult time adjusting to the noisy, and nosy Fisher household. Put yourself in her shoes for a moment, imagine growing up mostly alone, with almost no parental supervision. Would you resent the shocking change and sudden shift from independence to forced dependance?

2) Have you ever been in a situation where you found a dear friend or someone you could imagine marrying, only to lose them suddenly? How did/would you handle such a shock?

3) Now put yourself in Zeke's position. In today's world, taking responsibility often takes a backseat to personal wants, wishes and desires. Would you be so responsible in the same situation or would you pass the responsibility on to someone else?

4) Tobias left the family suddenly and has barely communicated with them in the five years since. If the same were true of a family member of yours, would you... could you forgive them so easily?

Would there remain a rift between you, even if you did try to forgive?

5) When Zeke invites Rebekah to Florida for his brother's wedding, do you think that will make things easier – or more difficult on the couple when they have to separate again?

Could they be courting danger, being together for such a short time, knowing they will have to be apart again for an undetermined amount of time?

If You haven't read BOOK ONE in the windy gap wishes series, don't miss it.

ABOUT THE PUBLISHER

Publishing for HIS Glory!

S&G Publishing offers books with messages that honor
Jesus Christ to the world! S&G works with Christian
authors to bring you the best in "inspirational" fiction
and non-fiction.

S&G is proud to publish a variety of genres:

inspirational romance

young reader

young adult

speculative

historical

suspense

Check out our website at

sgpublish.com

MORE FROM

S&G PUBLISHING

DON'T MISS NAOMI MILLER'S
AMISH SWEET SHOP SERIES